# 8 YEARS OF GLORY

## BARACK BECOMES A MOREHOUSE MAN

S. EARL WILSON, III

BALBOA.
PRESS
A DIVISION OF HAY HOUSE

Balboa Press books may be ordered through booksellers or by contacting:

Balboa Press
A Division of Hay House
1663 Liberty Drive
Bloomington, IN 47403
www.balboapress.com
1 (877) 407-4847

Print information available on the last page.

ISBN: 978-1-9822-1164-6 (sc)
ISBN: 978-1-9822-1166-0 (hc)
ISBN: 978-1-9822-1165-3 (e)

Library of Congress Control Number: 2018910589

Balboa Press rev. date: 12/07/2018

With special recognition to Henry M. Goodgame, Jr., class of 1984, for his complete dedication to Morehouse College, its name, its aims, achievements, and goals as Director of Alumni Relations. Much obliged!

Also, Special Thanks to:

Anthony Tetro of Dumont, New Jersey

Paul Toscano of New City, New York

Stephen Stallone of Clayton, California

Grazie!

# CONTENTS

# INTRODUCTION

My mother attended Clark College in Atlanta, Georgia for two years, then married my father who was a student at Morehouse College. She never finished, but he did – graduating in 1929 with honors. My father's mother, my grandmother, possessed a brilliant mind and was allowed to gain a high school diploma by her Caucasian kin folks. A noticeable feat in those days when very few Negroes could even read and figure. All three of them became school teachers. Needless to say, they all played a significant part in my life. Each of them taught me quotes and words of great writers and thinkers of which I apply to other great people, one in particular, President Barack Obama.

From my mother, Longfellow:

> "Lives of great men all remind us
> We can make our lives sublime
> And, departing, leave behind us
> Footprints on the sands of time
> Footprints, that perhaps another.
> Sailing o'er life's solemn main
> A forlorn and shipwrecked brother
> Seeing shall take heart again."

From my grandmother, Edgar Guest:

> "Somebody said that it couldn't be done
> But he with a chuckle replied
> That "maybe it couldn't," but he would be one
> Who wouldn't say so till he tried.
> So he buckled right in with the trace of a grin
> On his face. If he worried he hid it.

He started to sing as he tackled the thing
That couldn't be done, and he did it.
Somebody scoffed: "Oh, you'll never do that;
At least no Black man ever has done it";
But he took off his coat and he took off his hat,
And the first we knew he'd begun it.
With a lift of his chin and a bit of a grin,
Without any doubting or quiddit
He started to sing as he tackled the thing
That couldn't be done, and HE DID IT!"

May I add - "He shole did."

My father – Ella W. Wilcox:

"One ship drives east, another drives west,
With the self same wind that blows.
'Tis the set of the sails
And not the gales
That tells us the way to go."

Myself – William Cowper:

"Fleecy locks and black complexion
Cannot forfeit nature's claim
Skins may differ but affection
Dwells in white and black the same."

May I also add: His complexion was not ebony nor his hair nappy.

# AS AN INSPIRATION FOR AFRO/ AMERICAN YOUTH

I quote myself again:

## SUPPOSES

Little black children playing ring around the roses,

I wonder what are your supposes?

If you graduate from the University of Alabama,

Do you suppose you could become another Barack Obama?

If you finish Georgia Tech with joy,

Could you become another Elijah McCoy?

Suppose you finish Morehouse College and get your graduation ring,

Would you become another Martin Luther King?

Suppose you are from Washington, D.C.

And you went to Tuskegee.

Could you become another Washington

Like George Carver and Booker T. Washington?

Suppose you are from the city of the Kentucky Derby,

Could you attend Paine college in Augusta

And become another Frank Yerby?

If you studied dramatics at the school of Yale,

Could you become another Denzel (Washington)?

How about studying at Tennessee State and not being a loafer.

Suppose you could be another Oprah?

Mississippi's Congressman Bennie Thompson finished Tougaloo

Could this, perhaps, in the future be you?

There are thousands of things that you can be

It's all up to you and me.

You to make up your mind

And me to see that you don't fall behind!

What about me, the author, and why do I write? I have a meticulous, sensitive, demanding attitude about children and adult learning and reading. In some school districts, black children do not seem to do well in the reading categories.

## MINORITIES READING AND LEARNING

Local Hattiesburg author and retired school teacher (40 years), Samuel Earl Wilson III, believes that black students take a greater interest in reading and learning when the books that they read include black people, events, environments, and things that they can relate to. Quoted from his poem *Ordinary Black People*,

> Say something positive about "The Hood,"
> Then cross on over to Hollywood.
> Show Morgan Freeman doing Macbeth
> Or Denzel Washington as King Lear.
> Halle Berry as the Queen of Sheba
> Or Oprah Winfrey in *The Color Purple*.
> It's all in the same circle.
> For opera advice, use Leontyne Price.

Wilson's letter to local and national school districts, the United States Secretary of Education, Dr. Arne Duncan, and Mississippi's Superintendent of Education, Dr. Lynn J. House:

Dear Sir or Madam:

Are we still under the illusion that all races of mankind learn the same way or alike? The white literacy sets the standards to our tests. Surely some Africans and African Americans do well on these tests, even "Yours truly" (this writer). But we are the exceptions, not the rule. Most black students cannot, or will not, relate to non-ebony characters or situations. How can they relate to these characters: Little Miss Muffett, Peter Pan, Jack and the Beanstalk,

The Cat in the Hat, Cinderella, Snow White, Little Boy Blue, Peter, Peter, the Pumpkin Eater?

How about Little Black Boy and Little Black Girl, The Opossum Up the Persimmon Tree, or Walter, Walter the Watermelon Stalker?

Can a kid from the black ghetto better relate to *Alice in Wonderland* or "Aunt Jemima in the Kitchen?" Would they prefer to read *Harry Potter* rather than *For the Young at Heart?* Of course you would have to read them both before giving me your opinion.

After reading these books, *For the Young at Heart, Just Stories for the Young,* and *It's Cotton Blossom Time,* I would appreciate your opinion.

What are the merits of black authors such as Richard Wright, Zora Neale Hurston, Margaret Walker, James Baldwin, or S. Earl Wilson, III? Are you willing to take a step forward and initiate materials that Black students can relate to, or do you prefer to maintain the status quo and continue to drift along like a tumbleweed in a ghost town?

A title after your name (Ph. D.) does not mean anything if Johnnie never learns to read.

Respectfully yours,

S. Earl Wilson, III

When I was a child, I thought as a child. I read as children do or did the literature given to me to read. My concepts and values were formed as my imagination soared into the heavens along with Peter Pan and the cow that jumped over the moon. Way up yonder, doves could fly and so could little white fairies and beyond. I loved Mary's little lambs, Little Bo Peep's sheep and all the kings horses that attempted to assist Humpty Dumpty.

When I went to Chicago, I wondered if the tall buildings I saw were as tall as Jack's beanstalk? I also wondered if the beautiful black girls that I saw, even the Creoles in New Orleans, were as beautiful as Cinderella or Snow White? No, no, impossible! I knew Little Miss Muffett and about her tuffett; Little Red Riding Hood; Little Boy Blue, who was white; and Mary, Mary, though contrary, could grow plants. I learned all of this and more, even though it did not relate to the world I lived in or my environment.

I'm a Negro. The only things I ever read then about Colored folks were Little Black Sambo; Ten Little Niggers; Jim, the escaped slave, in Mark Twain's *Tom Sawyer*; and *Black Boy* by Richard Wright. I had a long way to go before I learned that Black was also beautiful.

I was a Negro and still am, I guess, unless you want to say that I am Afro/American, Black or Colored. Use whatever terminology you choose. Just be assured that I am not Caucasian or Asian, even though genes of both intermingle in my hereditary system.

Get my book *Just Stories for the Young/The Boyyer Series*. It instills pride and beauty into the minds of Black children, teenagers and adults, both Young and Old (8 – 108)!

S. E. Wilson, III

# ONE OR SOME OF SAM WILSON'S BOOKS

*ᴍ*

Any of my books would be a great present to/for:

1. You and you alone if you love Sam Wilson
2. Your loquacious spouse who like an old
refrigerator - "Can't Keep Nothing"
3. Your very smart offsprings who like to read and
watch the History Channel and Jeopardy
4. Grandparents who like to eat pickles and roasted asparagus
5. Friends who enjoy jokes and humor and
laugh their asses off for nothingness
6. Those whom you would like to impress, to show them something
7. Unfortunate people who can't afford the price of a good book
8. Kin-folks who never finished college and those with
Ph. D.s to show that you love them the same.
9. Cantankerous cousins who think they know it all
10. Anybody, for any reason: Christmas, Birthday,
Graduation, Promotion, Love, Honor, and Respect!

S. Earl Wilson, III
997 Richburg Road
Hattiesburg, MS 39402
Phone: (601) 261-9599

*Free delivery within a radius of 60 miles and free postage otherwise*

# HIS BOOKS TO CHOOSE FROM

*The Jitney Man – Mississippi Stories – 8 Years of Glory*

*100 Miles from New Orleans – For the Young at
Heart – Memoirs of a Morehouse Man*

*Fools, Fun, Folks, Facts, and Fiction – Fantastic
Short, Short Stories and Tales*

*The Possum Hunter – It's Cotton Blossom Time –
Just Stories for the Young – The Ghetto Poet*

## ENJOY!

# A MAN AND HIS BOOKS

$\sim m \sim$

I write for Negroes, Colored Folks, and Niggers. I also write for white folks and red necks just above the poverty level who have the ability to read. I do not write for Islanders, for Afro-Americans, Caucasians, Europeans, WASPS, or Asians because neither of these have the background to comprehend my style and poetic hyperbole.

Think I'm not sincere? Do you know what "Play Lacking" is? Do you understand "Swimming in the head?" What does "fixin' to be" mean? See what I mean!

Also, I am unwilling to be held down by facts. My mind wanders to and fro. People born in the ghettos, on farms, plantations or in the country who have elevated themselves through education could be the exceptions to my rules. They perhaps, can follow me, providing they are not caught up in their superficial intellectual worlds.

You know I'm a fan of the Temptations – not the new ones but the old original ones. What does this have to do with today's ventures – Mississippi writings? You see, their greatest lead singer was David Ruffin who was from Meridian, Mississippi. His words inspired me like, "I can turn the gray skies blue," "I can make it rain whenever I want it to," or "It was just my imagination running away with me – just my imagination running – away – with me!"

When I am at my desk alone at my home in Mississippi with my pen in my hand, my imagination just doesn't run, it sometimes soars past the speed of light then trickles to the drop of a slow leaking faucet with moments of moderation in between. What can I do? I seem to be unlimited. My mind is free to compose, free to wander, free to write about anything that I choose. *Boo Boo, Dough Dough, Wee Wee – The Jitney Man, Preachers, Teachers, Doctors, Lawyers, the Supernatural. I can make things fly like birds in the sky. I can make myself fly! I can create rain, thunder, tornadoes, hurricanes or sprinkles, or gentle breezes. I can love, hate, build or destroy. Whatever I choose.*

These are the prerogatives of a fiction writer. Non-fiction writers cannot enjoy this freedom. They are limited by truth, facts – restricted to relaying things just as they are or were not how they would have them to be. They must tell the world exactly how Adolph Hitler was or how Osama bin Laden is. They cannot cover them up with glory. Unlike me, I can transform beasts into beauties, ugly ducklings into swans, a Mississippi homeboy into a Minnesota or Cape Cod hero.

If Abe Lincoln was ugly, he was ugly. There is nothing you can write to the contrary. But I can make my characters ugly or beautiful, tall or short, naked or clothed, winsome or foolish.

There is no greater freedom than writing. If you are a non-fiction writer, then you enjoy the expressions of telling the truth. I can see why, now those who were imprisoned could write so well. Their bodies were jailed but their minds were free, the apostle Paul, for example, but he wrote facts. Unlike him, I am unwilling to be held down by facts. Writing about President Barack Obama was both a challenge and a thrill, with no exaggerations, only the truth.

My books are dedicated to YOU!

You can follow the sequences of my mind through patterns of obscurities, and ambiguous places and scenes; tolerate my profanity and obscene expressions; cry with me in inhumane acts and brutality on mankind; laugh when laughter is merited at things that are laughable and comical. You, who will ride, run or walk with me through narrow paths and widen streets, march through the valleys of death to the avenues of life – to hell and back again. You who can dream and imagine and like to read my writings!

These books are dedicated to you and you alone! You, You and nobody else but You!

If you finished the third grade and can read, welcome to my world.

S. Earl Wilson, III

# 8 YEARS OF GLORY

*◆◆◆*

"F— Barack Obama," I said. "Forget him. Who does he think he is, invading my life which is already filled with black heroes?"

I'm a Morehouse man, and so was my father before me; so was Martin Luther King, Jr. and his father before him. I always thought that if any black scholar should become President of the United States, of America, it would be a Morehouse College graduate. Nobody else is qualified. In my eyesight, Barack, although seemingly perspicuous in his prose, handsome and well learned, still was not a Morehouse man then, at that time. Why am I so predisposed and adamant about Morehouse graduates, men of eminence, grandeur, and magnificence? Look at these:

## ACADEMIA

| NAME | CLASS YEAR | NOTABILITY |
|---|---|---|
| Mordecai Wyatt Johnson | 1911 | First African-American President of Howard University |
| Russell L. Adams | 1952 | Chair, Department Afro American Studies, Howard University (1971-2005); Professor Emeritus, Howard University |
| Benjamin Brawley | 1901 | First Dean of Morehouse College |

| | | |
|---|---|---|
| Robert E. Johnson | 1982 | First African-American President of University of Massachusetts Dartmouth and Becker College |
| Calvin O. Butts | 1972 | President, SUNY College at Old Westbury; Pastor, Abyssinian Baptist Church |
| Ronald L. Carter | 1971 | President, Johnson C. Smith University; former Dean of Students Boston University and the University of the Witwaterstrand in South African-American |
| Charles D. Churchwell | 1952 | Former Dean of Library Services at Washington University in St. Louis; Brown University and Miami University (OH) |
| James A. Colston | 1932 | 2nd President, Bethune-Cookman University; President, Knoxville College; President, Savannah State University; 2nd President, Bronx Community College |
| Samuel Dubois Cook | 1948 | First Black Professor Emeritus and Trustee Emeritus at Duke University; President, Dillard University 1974-1997 |
| Guy C. Craft | 1951 | Former Dean of Library Services at Chicago State University; former Library Director at Robert W. |

| | | Woodruff Library of the Atlanta University Center and former Interim Dean of the School of Library and Information Studies at Clark Atlanta University |
| --- | --- | --- |
| Kevin Rome | 1989 | 16th President of Fisk University and 19th President of Lincoln University |
| Abraham L. Davis | 1961 | Distinguished Professor and Chair, Political Science Department, Morehouse College |
| Albert W. Dent | 1926 | President of Dillard University. Chief Executive of Flint-Goodridge Hospital, advocate for education and healthcare of impoverished people |
| James C. Early | 1969 | Distinguished Director of Cultural Heritage Policy at the Smithsonian Institution Center for Folklife and Cultural Heritage, Washington, D.C. |
| Eddie Claude | 1989 | Chair, Center for African American Studies and Professor at Princeton University; guest contributor: *The Tavis Smiley Show* |
| Marshall Grigsby | 1968 | Former President of Benedict College and former Vice President Provost and CEO of Hampton University |

| | | |
|---|---|---|
| William E. Holmes | | Former President of Central City College, faculty of the Atlanta Baptist Institute for 25 years |
| John Hopps, Jr. | 1958 | Former Director of the Charles Stark Draper Laboratory and Distinguished Physics Professor at the Massachusetts Institute of Technology; recipient of the Materials Advancement Award |
| David Jones | 1983 | Vice President of Human Resources, Stanford University |
| Walter J. Leonard | | Former Assistant Dean, Harvard Law School; former President of Fisk University; two fellowships are named in his honor at Oxford University |
| James Nabrit, Jr. | 1923 | Second African-American President of Howard University and former Deputy of United Nations Ambassador |
| Calvin Mackie | 1990 | Former Professor of Engineering, Tulane University; winner of the 2003 Presidential Award for Excellence in Science, Mathematics, and Engineering; Black Engineer of the Year for College Level Educators |

| | | |
|---|---|---|
| Walter E. Massey | 1958 | President, School of the Art Institute of Chicago; former Professor of Physics at the University of Chicago; former Dean of the College of Physics at Brown University; former Provost of the University of California System; President Emeritus at Morehouse College |
| Richard McKinney | 1931 | First African-American President of Storer College; former Dean at Virginia Union University and Morgan State University |
| Richard J. Powell | 1975 | Distinguished Professor of Art History at Duke University; editor-in-chief, the Art Bulletin; Wilbur Lucius Cross Medalist, Yale University Alumni of the Year Award |
| Ronald S. Sullivan, Jr. | 1989 | First African-American Faculty Dean, Harvard College. Professor, Harvard Law School and Director of the Criminal Justice Institute at Harvard Law; legal analyst at CNN, Fox News |
| James F. Williams | | Current Dean of Libraries, University of Colorado at Boulder, 2002 Melvil Dewey Medal recipient |
| Charles V. Willie | 1948 | Distinguished Professor Emeritus, Harvard University Graduate School of Education |

| John S. Wilson, Jr. | 1979 | Executive Director of the White House Initiative on Historically Black Colleges and Universities; former Assistant Provost at the Massachusetts Institute of Technology |
| Dr. Jackson B. Sheftall, Ed.D., Ed.S. | 1954 | Retired lead psychologist, Bibb City Board of Education, Macon, GA |

## BUSINESS

| Nathaniel H. Bronner, Sr. | 1940 | Founder and former CEO, Bronner Bros., which is also the publisher of *Upscale Magazine* |
| Ronald D. Brown | | Former CEO, Atlanta Life Financial Group, Inc. |
| Herman Cain | 1967 | Former CEO, Godfather's Pizza |
| Emmett Carson | 1981 | CEO and President, Silicon Valley Community Foundation |
| James W. Compton | 1961 | Board of Directors, Ariel Investments, Inc.; retired President and CEO, Chicago Urban League |
| Reginald E. Davis | 1984 | President, RBC Bank, former Senior Executive, Wachovia; named one of the "75 Most Powerful African-Americans in Corporate America" by *Black Enterprise* magazine |

| Paul Q. Judge | 1998 | Noted entrepreneur and scholar |
| Russell Ewing | 1991 | Executive Director, SEI Investments Company |
| Dale E. Jones | 1982 | Vice Chair, Heidrick & Struggles International, Inc. |
| Robert L. Mallett | 1979 | Former Vice President, Pfizer Corporation, President Pfizer Foundation/Member of Accordia Global Health Foundation's Board of Directors |
| Walter E. Massey | 1958 | Former Chairman, Bank of America; former Director of the National Science Foundation |
| Kent Matlock | 1986 | CEO of Matlock Advertising & Public Relations |
| John W. Mims | 1982 | Sr. Vice President Starwood Hotels & Resorts Worldwide |
| Arthur E. Johnson | 1968 | Former President and COO, Lockheed Martin I&SS, and President, IBM, FSC Division |

| Ronald L. Mimms | 1956 | Among the first African-American executive level managers at IBM. Director of the Transition Program – a program he developed to assist underachieving first year students of color at NC State University. |
| Rufus H. Rivers | 1986 | Managing Director, RLJ Equity Partners, Board of Directors; Thomas & Betts, the National Association of Investment Companies (NAIC) |
| Robert T. Ross | 1981 | Director, NJ Wealth Management Banking at Merrill Lynch |
| Maceo K. Sloan | 1971 | Chair and CEO NCM Capital Management Group; Chair and CEO Sloan Financial Group, Inc., Board of Directors, SCANA Corporation |
| Karim Webb | | American restaurateur |
| Vern Perry | 1994 | Co-Head of Strategic Partners |

## ENTERTAINMENT

### <u>MUSIC</u>

| Saul Williams | 1994 | Performing artist and actor |

| Uzee Brown, Jr. | 1972 | Opera singer, composer |
| Byron Cage | 1987 | Grammy-nominated gospel singer; NAACP-Image Award nominee; winner of six Stellar Awards |
| Stephen "Zumbi" | 1995 | Rapper, founder of Zion I Gaines |
| Anthony "Amp Live" Anderson | 1995 | Producer, founder of Zion I |
| JohnJason Cecil | 1995 | Blues Artist, founder of The Bush League |
| Keith "Guru" Elam | 1983 | Rapper, founder of Gang Starr |
| Edmund Jenkins | 1914 | Harlem Renaissance composer; studied under Kemper Harreld |
| Canton Jones | 1985 | Grammy-nominated gospel singer |
| Martin Luther McCoy | 1992 | Musician and actor |
| Dr. David Edward Morrow | 1980 | Morehouse College Glee Club Director |
| Babatunde Olatunji | 1954 | Grammy-Award winning Nigerian drummer; social activist and recording artist; *Drums of Passion* |
| Shakir Stewart | 1996 | Senior Vice President of Island Def Jam Music Group; Executive Vice President of Def Jam |

P J Morton                          Maroon 5 keyboardist


## FILM, TELEVISION, AND THEATER

| Samuel L. Jackson | 1972 | Actor |

| Kevin A. Ross | 1985 | Host/producer of daytime syndication legal show *America's Court with Judge Ross* |

| Stu James | 1989 | Broadway and television actor; *Color Purple, Dreamgirls, All My Children, General Hospital* |

| Erik King | 1985 | Actor, *Dexter* |

| Spike Lee | 1979 | Film director and producer |

| Seith Mann | 1995 | Television director: *The Wire, Grey'sAnatomy*; winner of the NAACP Image Award |

| Bill G. Nunn III | 1976 | Actor, *School Daze, Mo Better Blues, New Jack City* |

| Avery O. Williams | 1986 | Screenwriter; *Notes In A Minor Key, Re-Directing Eddie* |

| Fonzworth Bentley | 1997 | Well-known media personality |

| Rockmond Dunbar | | Actor, *Soul Food, Girlfriends* |

| Brian Tyree Henry | 2004 | Actor, *Atlanta* (TV series) |

# Government, Law And Public Policy

## FEDERAL GOVERNMENT

| | | |
|---|---|---|
| Nate Bennett-Fleming | 2007 | Shadow U.S. Representative for the District of Columbia |
| Sanford Bishop | 1968 | U.S. Congressman (Georgia) |
| John Brewer | 1989 | Associate Administrator, Foreign Agricultural Services and General Sales Manager, United States Department of Agriculture |
| James H. Shelton III | 1989 | Former Deputy Secretary of Education for the United States |
| Julies E. Coles | 1964 | Former U.S. Ambassador to Senegal; former President of Africare |
| George Haley | 1949 | Former Chair U.S. Postal Rate Commission and Ambassador to the Republic of Ghana; brother to Alex Haley |
| James L. Hudson | 1961 | Director of the European Bank for Reconstruction and Development; Chair, National Capitol Revitalization Corporation Board |
| Earl F. Hilliard | 1964 | Former U.S. Congressman (Alabama) |
| John Hopps, Jr. | 1958 | Former Deputy Under Secretary United States Department of Defense |

| | | |
|---|---|---|
| Howard E. Jeter | 1970 | Former U.S. Ambassador to Nigeria; former U.S. Ambassador to Botswana |
| Robert L. Mallett | 1979 | Former Deputy Secretary of Commerce U.S. Department of Commerce; VP Pfizer Corporation, President Pfizer Foundation |
| James Nabrit, Jr. | 1923 | Former Deputy U.S. Ambassador to the United Nations; second African-Americans President of Howard University |
| Major R. Owens | 1956 | U.S. Congressman (New York) |
| Cedric Richmond | 1995 | U.S. Congressman (Louisiana) |
| David Satcher | 1963 | 16th U.S. Surgeon General, former President of Morehouse School of Medicine |
| Joel Secundy | 1993 | Deputy Assistant Secretary, Services Industries, International Trade Administrations, United States Department of Commerce |
| Louis W. Sullivan | 1954 | Former U.S. Secretary of Health and Human Services and current President Emeritus of Morehouse School of Medicine |

| Horace T. Ward | 1927 | First African-American to challenge the racially discriminatory practices at the UGA School of Law; first African-American to be appointed to the United States District Court for the Northern District of Georgia; former member of the Georgia Senate |

## STATE GOVERNMENT

| Julian Bond | 1971 | Civil rights leader; former Georgia state representative and Chairman of the NAACP |
| Terrance Carroll | 1992 | Speaker, Colorado House of Representatives |
| Kenneth Dunkin | 1989 | Illinois House of Representatives |
| Jimmy Harris | | Member of the Louisiana House of Representatives for New Orleans since 2016 |
| Leroy Johnson | 1949 | Senator; first African- American elected to the Georgia General Assembly since Reconstruction |
| John Monds | 1987 | Highest number of votes received by any Libertarian candidate ever |
| Frank Peterman | 1985 | Florida House of Representatives |

| Bakari Sellers | 2005 | Youngest member elected to the South Carolina General Assembly |
| Sebastian Ridley-Thomas | 2009 | California State Assembly |
| Andre Thapedi | 1990 | Illinois House of Representatives |
| Perry Thurston, Jr. | 1982 | Florida House of Representatives S. Howard Woodson 1942 Bachelor of Divinity Morehouse School of Religion; former Speaker, New Jersey General Assembly |

## MAYORS

| Claude Black, Jr. | 1937 | First Black mayor Pro Tem San Antonio, Texas; civil rights leader; Pastor of Mt. Zion Baptist Church, San Antonio, Texas |
| Chuck Burris | 1971 | First Black mayor of Stone Mountain, Georgia |
| John Wesley Dobbs | 1897 | The unofficial "Mayor" of Sweet Auburn Avenue (1937- 1949); Civic Leader and co- founder of the Atlanta Negro Voters League |
| Maynard Jackson | 1956 | First Black mayor of Atlanta, Georgia; Jackson served three terms as Mayor; founder and CEO of Jackson Securities, Inc.; National Development Chair, Democratic National Committee |

| Ed McIntyre | 1956 | First African-American mayor of Augusta, Georgia |
| Alvin Parks, Jr. | 1983 | Mayor, East St. Louis, Illinois (2007-present) |
| James O. Webb | 1953 | Mayor, Glencoe, Illinois; established the first HMO in Illinois and served as Chair, President and CEO of the Dental Network of America (of the Health Care Service Corporation) |
| Clinton I. Young | 1972 | Mayor, Mt. Vernon, New York (2008-present) |

## JUDGES AND LAWYERS

| Michael D. Carter | 1986 | Judge, Superior Court, Los Angeles County |
| George W. Crockett, Jr. | 1931 | Former U.S. Congressman, United States Congress; Founding Member of the National Lawyer's Guild; Co-founded the first racially integrated law firm in the U.S.; first Black attorney in the U.S. Department of Laboratory |
| Ralph B. Everett | 1973 | President and CEO, Joint Center for Political and Economic Studies |
| Joseph Jerome Farris | 1951 | Justice, United States Court of Appeals 9th Circuit |

| Robert V. Franklin | 1947 | Retired Judge, Ohio District Court of Appeals |
| Calvin S. Graves | 1973 | Chief Judge, Atlanta Municipal Court, Atlanta, Georgia |
| Odell Horton | 1951 | Justice, U.S. District Court, W. Tennessee |
| Reginald C. Lindsay | 1967 | Justice, United States Court of Appeals 7th Circuit |
| James L. Hudson | 1961 | Director of the European Bank for Reconstruction and Development; Chair, National Capitol Revitalization Corporation Board |
| Michael D. Johnson | 1990 | Judge, Superior Court, Fulton Co., Georgia |
| Jeh Johnson | 1979 | Secretary of Homeland Security; first Black partner, Paul, Weiss, Rifkind, Wharton, & Garrison, LLP; named to the National Law Journal's 50 Most Influential Minority Lawyers; appointed General Counsel for the Defense Department by President Barack Obama; former General Counsel U.S. Air Force |
| C. Vernon Mason | 1967 | Disbarred lawyer, Tawana Brawley case, Howard Beach incident |

| Stephen L. Maxwell | 1942 | First Black District Court Judge in Minnesota |
| Tyrone C. Means | 1973 | Founding Partner, Thomas, Means, Gillis, & Seay; Counsel and Board Member, Martin Luther King, Jr. National Memorial Project Foundation |
| Graham T. Perry | c. 1920 | First African American Assistant Attorney-General for State of Illinois |
| Olu Stevens | 1992 | Circuit Court Judge for the 30th Circuit, Kentucky |
| Thomas Sampson, Sr. | 1968 | Founding partner of Thompson, Kennedy, Sampson, & Patterson, the oldest minority-owned law firm in the state of Georgia |
| Jerome Walker | 1981 | Partner, Troutman Sanders, LLP; former General Counsel for the Hong Kong & Shanghai Banking Corp, LTD |
| Horace T. Ward | 1949 | Federal Judge, U.S. District Court Northern Georgia; inducted into the National Bar Association Hall of Fame; recipient of the Trumpet Award for Civil Rights Advocacy |

| Brent Wilson | 1973 | Partner, Elarbee, Thompson, Sapp & Wilson; Who's Who in American law; listed among America's Top Black Lawyers by *Black Enterprise*; Chamber's USA Best Lawyers for Business |
| Richard T. White | 1967 | Sr. VP and General Counsel for the Auto Club Group and Chairman of the Association of Corporate Counsel |
| Don Clendon | 1956 | Attorney. New York Mets Baseball and 1969 World Series MVP |
| Willie Davis | 1956 | Attorney. Football and track, Morehouse, and Judge |
| Jose Ananias | 1951 | Educator, New York Board of Education |
| Ozro Thaddeus Wells | 1953 | Attorney, JD, New York, NY |
| Howard Moore | 1954 | Attorney and civil rights activist |
| Clifton E. Hall, Jr. | | Attorney, NYC. Football, Morehouse |

## JOURNALIST AND MEDIA PERSONALITIES

| Geoff Bennett | 2002 | Washington reporter, Time Warner Cable News/NY1 |

| Michael DeMond Davis | 1961 | Pulitizer Prize-nominated journalist; author of *Black American Women in Olympic Track & Field* and co-author of *Thurgood Marshall: Warrior at the Bar, Rebel on the Bench* |
| Robert E. Johnson | 1948 | Former Executive Editor and Associate Publisher, *Jet Magazine* |
| Jamal Simmons | 1993 | Political correspondent for CNN |
| Vincent Tubbs Negro | c. 1938 | Co-founder of National Newspaper Week and first African American to head a motion picture industry union |

## LITERATURE

| Lerone Bennett, Jr. | 1949 | Senior editor for the Johnson Publishing Group (*JET, Ebony*); author of *Before the Mayflower* Sanford Biggers 1993 Artist, professor Columbia University School of the Arts |
| Thomas Dent | 1952 | Writer and poet; author of *Magnolia Street* |
| Jefferson Grisby | 1938 | Author, artist; NAACP Man of the Year Award; first African American to publish a book for collegiate art teachers |
| Miles Marshall Lewis | 1993 | Pop culture critic, essayist, and author |

| Samuel Earl Wilson, III | 1955 | Author, *Memoirs of a Morehouse Man, It's Cotton Blossom Time, The Possum Hunter* |
| --- | --- | --- |
| Donald P. Stone | 1957 | Freelance writer/publisher, *Fallen Prince* |
| Dr. Ira E. (Syracuse) Harrison, Ph.D. | 1955 | Professor Emeritus, University of Tennessee, Department of Anthropology, Knoxville, TN. Afro-American poet. |

## MILITARY SERVICE

| Otha Thornton, Lt. Colonel | 1989 | 2013-2015 National President and Chairman of the Parent Teacher Association and also the first African- American male elected. President in the history of the association. Former Director of Human Resources and Presidential Communications Agency; awarded an Honorary Doctorate degree by Michigan Technological University; former Assistant Professor, Michigan Technological University; winner of the Parting of the Waters Award for Faculty Excellence |
| --- | --- | --- |
| James R. Hall, | 1957 | Deputy Inspector General, the United Lt. General (ret.) States Army |

## RELIGION

| | | |
|---|---|---|
| Fred C. Lofton | 1953 | Metropolitan Baptist Church, Memphis, TN |
| Harrison N. Bouey | 1873 | Pastor and missionary |
| Amos C. Brown | 1964 | Pastor, Third Baptist Church of San Francisco; President, San Francisco branch of NAACP-Image |
| M. William Howard, Jr. | 1968 | Pastor, Bethany Baptist Church; former President, New York Theological Seminary; Chair, Rutgers University Board of Governors |
| Thomas Kilgore, Jr. | 1931 | Civil rights pioneer and Pastor Emeritus, Second Baptist Church; a building is named in his honor on the Morehouse campus |
| Otis Moss, Jr. | 1956 | Pastor and theologian |
| Otis Moss, III | 1992 | Pastor, Trinity United Church of Christ; listed on the Root 100 |
| Kelly Miller Smith | 1942 | Assistant dean, Vanderbilt University Divinity School (circa 1970s-1980s) |
| Keith L. Somerville | 1992 | Founding Pastor, One Life United Methodist Churchwell |
| Howard Thurman | 1923 | Renowned theologian; Dean of Chapel Boston University |

| Frederick B. Williams | | Canon of the Church of the Intercession in Harlem, New York (1971-2005) |
|---|---|---|

## SCIENCE AND MEDICINE

| Henry W. Foster, Jr. | 1954 | President Emeritus, Meharry Medical College; clinical professor, Vanderbilt University; former nominee to post of U.S. Surgeon General; presidential advisor |
|---|---|---|
| Corey Hebert | 1991 | Celebrity physician; radio talk show host; Chief Medical Editor of National Broadcasting Company for the Gulf Coast; first Black Chief Resident of Pediatrics at Tulane University; Chief Executive Officer of Community Health TV |
| John Hopps, Jr. | 1958 | Physicist; former longtime Director of the Charles Stark Draper Laboratory and distinguished professor at the Massachusetts Institute of Technology (MIT); recipient of the National Materials Advancement Award; former Deputy Under Secretary for the United States Department of Defense |
| Roger Wood, II | 1966 | Computer scientist; first African-American software developer at Bell Labs |

| Calvin B. Johnson | 1989 | 24th Secretary of Health for the Commonwealth of Pennsylvania of the Pennsylvania Department of Health |
| --- | --- | --- |
| Paul Q. Judge | 1998 | Award-winning computer technologist, inventor, and entrepreneur; recipient of MIT Technology Review Magazine's "100 Top Innovators under 35"; voted Black Engineer of the Year (2006) |
| Samuel M. Nabrit | 1925 | Distinguished science professor; first African- American appointed to the U.S. Atomic Energy Commission; served on Dwight Eisenhower's National Science Board; first African-American to receive a doctoral degree from Brown University; first African-American to serve as Trustee at Brown University; President of Texas Southern University |
| Donald Hopkins | 1962 | Director and Vice President, Health Programs, the Carter Center; a 1995 MacArthur Fellow; nominated for the Pulitzer Prize in 1983 |
| William D. Hutchinson | 1955 | Rocket and laser scientist, Boeing Dept., Rocketdyne |
| James King | 1953 | Professor and intern department chair of chemistry, Morehouse Colleges |

| | | |
|---|---|---|
| Judge N. King | 1957 | Chemist, physical and organic; MBA; airman; pilot |
| Roderic Pettigrew | 1972 | Cardiologist and renowned biomedical engineer; Director, National Institute of Biomedical Imaging and Bioengineering; former Director of magnetic Resonance Research and Professor of Radiology and Cardiology at Emory University School of Medicine; listed annually among the "Best Doctors in America" |
| Mack Roach III | 1975 | Chair, Radiation Oncology, University of California, San Francisco; named four times among the "Best Doctors in America"; American Cancer Society Fellow; American College of Radiology Fellow |
| Asa G. Yancey, Sr. | 1937 | First African-American professor and Professor Emeritus at Emory University School of Medicine; first African-American doctor and Medical Director at Grady Memorial Hospital |
| Charles DeWitt Watts | 1938 | First board-certified African-Americans surgeon in North Carolina; founder of Lincoln Community Health Center |

## SERVICE AND SOCIAL REFORM

Jerome Boger

Current referee and umpire in the NFL (National Football League); former quarterback for the Morehouse Tigers football team

Caesar "Zip" Gayles     1924

Former head football coach and former head basketball coach at Langston University; member of SWAC Hall of Fame and NAIA Basketball Hall of Fame

David Graham     1982

DE, Seattle Seahawks, 1982- 1987

Ramon Harewood     2010

OL, Baltimore Ravens, 2010

Issac Keys

LB, Arizona Cardinals, 2004- 2005

John David Washington     2006

RB, St. Louis Rams, 2006; all- time leading rusher at Morehouse; RB in the UFL; son of Oscar Award-winning actor Denzel Washington

## OTHERS

John Sharpe James     1992

US Army Major, decorated veteran, member of Municipal Council of Newark

Dexter King

Son of Martin Luther King, Jr.

Ennis Cosby     1992

Son of comedian Bill Cosby

| | | |
|---|---|---|
| Benjamin F. Logan, Sr. | 1960 | Retired Accountant, GM Corporation, Atlanta, GA. Creator of events that added money and finances to Morehouse's athletics substantially and abundantly |
| Larry G. McFarland | 1959 | Spec., P. G. County Govt., HCD Landover Mall, Landover, MD |
| Joshua Packwood | 2008 | First white valedictorian of Morehouse |
| William K. Dease | 1954 | Registrar, Morehouse College Retired Announcer great booming voice of Jackson State University (MS) and Morehouse College (GA) football games. He possessed one of the greatest speaking, voices, sounds produced by vibration of the vocal cords as heard in vowels and consonants at Athletic and other events at Jackson State University and Morehouse College. |

## NOTABLE FACULTY

| NAME | DEPARTMENT | NOTABILITY |
|---|---|---|
| Na'im Akbar | Psychology | Author, *Breaking the Chains and Images of Psychological Slavery* |
| Amalia Amaki | History | Modern and contemporary artist |

| | | |
|---|---|---|
| Clayborne Carson | History | Executive Director, Martin Luther King, Jr. Collection; professor, Stanford University |
| Lawrence Edward Carter | Religion | Dean, Martin Luther King Chapel; Fulbright Scholar; founder of the Ghandi-King-Ikeda Community Builders Prize |
| Claude B. Dansby | Mathematics | Chair, Mathematics Department |
| Louis Delsarte | Fine Arts | Painter, muralist |
| E. Franklin Frazier | Sociology | Author, *Black Bourgeoisie* |
| Kemper Harreld | Music | Established the Morehouse College Glee Club |
| J. K. Haynes | Biology | Chair, Biology Department; New York Academy of Science; Who's Who in Science and Engineering; Who's Who Among America's Teachers; Visiting Scholar, Brown University |
| John Hope | President | First Black president of Morehouse |
| John Hopps, Jr. | Physics | Former Director, Charles Stark Draper Laboratory, MIT |

| | | |
|---|---|---|
| Edward A. Jones | Foreign Language | Author, *A Candle in the Dark: A History of Morehouse Colleges* |
| Frederick E. Mapp | Mathematics | F. E. Mapp Science & Math Symposium |
| Benjamin E. Mays | President | Mentor to Martin Luther King, Jr.; established the institutions international academic reputation and gave rise to the Morehouse Mystique |
| Henry Cecil McBay | Chemistry | Winner of the Norton Prize in Chemistry, the Norris Award, and the Herty Award for Outstanding Contributions in Chemistry; first MLK Visiting Scholar at MIT |
| Charles Wilbert Snow | Political Science | Diplomat |
| Harriet J. Walton UNCF | Mathematics | "Mother Walton" was a Dana Fellow; Who's Who Men and Women of Science (1974); Who's Who of American |

Perhaps, in the future, the next Black President of the United States will be a Morehouse College graduate. Gradually, my prejudice began to dissipate after watching and listening to Barack Obama's voice in debates, speeches, and presentations. His mind was alert, his dialogue and reasoning articulate and transpicuous. This was no ordinary "dude." I began to remind myself that all of my idols were not Morehouse men – Michael Jordan, Elgin Baylor, Bill Russell, Joe Louis, Jackie Robinson, Laurence C. Jones (Piney

Woods School), nor Richard Wright went to Morehouse. Barack's mind was clever, brilliantly so. This superhuman was a "smart cookie."

His inauguration, Tuesday, January 20, 2009, as the first Black and 44th President of the United States of America, filled me with pride as I began to smile and simultaneously weep. Morehouse man or not, this man was a genius.

# PRESIDENT BARACK OBAMA'S INAUGURAL ADDRESS

## JANUARY 29, 2009

My fellow citizens: I stand here today humbled by the task before us, grateful for the trust you've bestowed, mindful of the sacrifices borne by our ancestors. I thank President Bush for his service to our nation as well as the generosity and cooperation he has shown throughout this transition.

Forty-four Americans have now taken the presidential oath. The words have been spoken during rising tides of prosperity and the still waters of peace. Yet, every so often, the oath is taken amidst gathering clouds and raging storms. At these moments, America has carried on not simply because of the skill of those in high office, but because we, the people, have remained faithful to the ideals of our forebears and true to our founding documents. So it has been; so it must be with this generation of Americans.

That we are in the midst of crisis is now well understood. Our nation is at war against a far-reaching network of violence and hatred. Our economy is badly weakened, a consequence of greed and irresponsiblity on the part of some, but also our collective failure to make hard choices and prepare the nation for a new age. Homes have been lost, jobs shed, businesses shuttered. Our health care is too costly, our schools fail too many – and each day brings further evidence that the ways we use energy strengthen our adversaries and threaten our planet. These are the indicators of crisis, subject to data and statistics. Less measurable, but no less profound, is a sapping of confidence across our land; a nagging fear that America's decline is inevitable, that the next generation must lower its sights.

Today I say to you that the challenges we face are real. They are serious and they are many. They will not be met easily or in a short span of time. But know this America: They will be met.

On this day, we gather because we have chosen hope over fear, unity of purpose over conflict and discord. On this day, we come to proclaim an end to the petty grievances and false promises, the recriminations and worn-out dogmas that for far too long have strangled our politics. We remain a young nation. But in the words of Scripture, the time has come to set aside childish things. The time has come to reaffirm our enduring spirit; to choose our better history; to carry forward that precious gift, that noble idea passed on from generation to generation; the God-given promise that all are equal, all are free, and all deserve a chance to pursue their full measure of happiness.

In reaffirming the greatness of our nation we understand that greatness is never a given. It must be earned. Our journey has never been one of short-cuts or settling for less. It has not been the path for the faint-hearted, for those that prefer leisure over work, or seek only the pleasures of riches and fame. Rather, it has been the risk-takers, the doers, the makers of things – some celebrated, but more often men and women obscure in their labor – who have carried us up the long rugged path towards prosperity and freedom.

For us, they packed up their few worldly possessions and traveled across oceans in search of a new life. For us, they toiled in sweatshops, and settled the West, endured the lash of the whip, and plowed the hard earth. For us, they fought and died in places like Concord and Gettysburg, Normandy and Khe Sahn.

Time and again these men and women struggled and sacrificed and worked till their hands were raw so that we might live a better life. They saw America as bigger than the sum of our individual ambitions, greater than all the differences of birth or wealth or faction.

This is the journey we continue today. We remain the most prosperous, powerful nation on Earth. Our workers are no less productive than when this crisis began. Our minds are no less inventive, our goods and services no less needed than they were last week, or last month, or last year. Our capacity remains undiminished. But our time of standing pat, of protecting narrow interests and putting off unpleasant decisions – that time has surely passed. Starting today, we must pick ourselves up, dust ourselves off, and begin again the work of remaking America.

For everywhere we look, there is work to be done. The state of the economy calls for action, bold and swift. And we will act, not only to create new jobs, but to lay a new foundation for growth. We will build the roads and bridges, the electric grids and digital lines that feed our commerce and bind us together. We'll restore science to its rightful place, and wield technology's wonders to raise health care's quality and lower its cost. We will harness the sun and the winds and the soil to fuel our cars and run our factories. And we will transform our schools and colleges and universities to meet the demands of a new age. All this we can do. All this we will do.

Now, there are some who question the scale of our ambitions, who suggest that our system cannot tolerate too many big plans. Their memories are short, for they have forgotten what this country has already done, what free men and women can achieve when imagination is joined to common purpose, and necessity to courage. What the cynics fall to understand is that the ground has shifted beneath them, that the stale political arguments that have consumed us for so long no longer apply.

The question we ask today is not whether our government is too big or too small, but whether it works — whether it helps families find jobs at a decent wage, care they can afford, a retirement that is dignified. Where the answer is yes, we intend to move forward. Where the answer is no, programs will end. And those of us who mange the public's dollars will be held to account, to spend wisely, reform bad habits, and do our business in the light of day, because only then can we restore the vital trust between a people and their government.

Nor is the question before us whether the market is a force for good or ill. Its power to generate wealth and expand freedom is unmatched. But this crisis has reminded us that without a watchful eye, the market can spin out of control. The nation cannot prosper long when it favors only the prosperous. The success of our economy has always depended not just on the size of our gross domestic product, but on the reach of our prosperity, on the ability to extend opportunity to every willing heart — not out of charity, but because it is the surest route to our common good.

As for our common defense, we reject as false the choice between our safety and our ideals. Our Founding Fathers, faced with perils that we can scarcely imagine, drafted a charter to assure the rule of law and the rights of man — a charter expanded by the blood of generations. Those ideals still light the world, and we will not give them up for expedience sake.

And so, to all the other peoples and governments who are watching today, from the grandest capitals to the small village where my father was born, know that America is a friend of each nation, and every man, woman and child who seeks a future of peace and dignity. And we are ready to lead once more.

Recall that earlier generations faced down fascism and communism not just with missiles and tanks, but with the sturdy alliances and enduring convictions. They understood that our power alone cannot protect us, nor does it entitle us to do as we please. Instead they knew that our power grows through its prudent use; our security emanates from the justness our cause, the force of our example, the tempering qualities of humility and restraint.

We are the keepers of this legacy. Guided by these principles once more we can meet those new threats that demand even greater effort, even greater cooperation and understanding between nations. We will begin to responsibly leave Iraq to its people and forge a hard-earned peace in Afghanistan. With old friends and old foes, we'll work tirelessly to lessen the nuclear threat, and roll back the specter of a warming planet.

We will not apologize for our way of life, nor will we waver in its defense. And for those who seek to advance their aims by inducing terror and slaughtering innocents, we say to you now that our spirit is stronger and cannot be broken – you cannot outlast us, and we will defeat you.

For we know that our patchwork heritage is a strength, not a weakness. We are a nation of Christians and Muslims, Jews and Hindus, and non-believers. We are shaped by every language and culture, drawn from every end of this Earth; and because we have tasted the bitter swill of civil war and segregation, and emerged from that dark chapter stronger and more united, we cannot help but believe that the old hatreds shall someday pass; that the lines of tribe shall soon dissolve; that as the world grows smaller, our common humanity shall reveal itself; and that America must play its role in ushering in a new era of peace.

To the Muslim world, we seek a new way forward, based on mutual interest and mutual respect. To those leaders around the globe who seek to sow conflict, or blame their society's ills on the West, know that your people will judge you on what you candidate build, not what you destroy.

To those who cling to power through corruption and deceit and the silencing of dissent, know that you are on the wrong side of history, but that we will extend a hand if you are willing to unclench your fist.

To the people of poor nations, we pledge to work alongside to you to make your farms flourish and let clean waters flow; to nourish starved bodies and feed hungry minds.

And to those nations like ours that enjoy relative plenty, we say we can no longer afford indifference to the suffering outside our borders, nor can we consume the world's resources without regard to effect. For the world has changed, and we must change with it.

As we consider the role that unfolds before us, we remember with humble gratitude those brave Americans who at this very hour patrol far-off deserts and distant mountains. They have something to tell us, just as the fallen heroes who lie in Arlington whisper through the ages.

We honor them not only because they are the guardians of our liberty, but because they embody the spirit of service – a willingness to find meaning in something greater than themselves.

And yet at this moment, a moment that will define a generation, it is precisely this spirit that must inhabit us all. For as much as government can do, and must do, it is ultimately the faith and determination of the American people upon which this nation relies. It is the kindness to take in a stranger when the levees break, the selflessness of workers who would rather cut their hours than see a friend lose their job which sees us through our darkest hours. It is the firefighter's courage to storm a stairway filled with smoke, but also a parent's willingness to nurture a child that finally decides our fate.

Our challenges may be new. The instruments with which we meet them may be new. But those values upon which our success depends – honesty and hard work, courage and fair play, tolerance and curiosity, loyalty and patriotism – these things are old. These things are true. They have been the quiet force of progress throughout our history.

What is demanded, then, is a return to these truths. What is required of us now is a new era of responsibility – a recognition on the part of every American that we have duties to ourselves, our nation and the world; duties that we do not grudgingly accept, but rather seize gladly, firm in the knowledge that there is nothing so satisfying to the spirit, so defining of our character than giving our all to a difficult task.

This is the price and the promise of citizenship. This is the source of our confidence – the knowledge that God calls on us to shape an uncertain destiny. This is the meaning of our liberty and our creed, why men and women and children of every race and faith can join in celebration across this magnificent mall; and why a man whose father less than 60 years ago might not have been served in a local restaurant can now stand before you to take a most sacred oath.

So let us mark this day with remembrance of who we are and how far we have traveled. In the year of America's birth, in the coldest of months, a small band of patriots huddled by dying campfires on the shores of an icy river. The capital was abandoned. The enemy was advancing. The snow was stained with blood. At the moment when the outcome of our revolution was most in doubt, the father our nation ordered these words to be read to the people:

> "Let it be told to the future world . . . that in the depth of winter, when nothing but hope and virtue could survive . . . that the city and country, alarmed at one common danger, came forth to meet [it]."

America: In the face of our common dangers, in this winter of our hardship, let us remember these timeless words. With hope and virtue, let us brave once more the icy currents, and endure what storms may come. Let it be said by our children's children that when we were tested we refused to let this journey end, that we did not turn back nor did we falter; and with eyes fixed on the horizon and God's grace upon us, we carried forth that great gift of freedom and delivered it safely to future generations.

Thank you. God bless you. And God bless the United States of America.

# INAUGURAL BALL

I was torn apart emotionally when he held his wife in his arms, and they eloquently floated on the dance floor to the song "At Last My Love Has Come Along" sung by Beyonce, not Etta James. It mattered not who the singer was. It could have been Etta James, Etta Jones, Sarah Vaughn, Billie Holiday or Ella Fitzgerald. It would not have mattered for nothing could obscure that graceful, magnificent, enchanted moment in history. If he could have held Dolly Madison or Martha Washington or Eleanor Roosevelt in his arms as he danced, nothing could replace the black beauty of Michelle. "Amen to that brother."

I feared for him as he and Michelle left their limousine and walked openly unescorted intermingling with the crowd of spectators. They had no fear, ever after knowing the ill fate of President John Kennedy on November 22, 1963. I felt sure that there were whites who envied and hated him but, let us not forget, that it was a black woman who stabbed Martin Luther King, Jr. in 1958 in New York. Amid danger and possible injury, the Obamas showed no fear and walked triumphantly with grace.

# HE BE PROUD

⌒⁁⌒

On his first day in office, President Obama reports to work at 8:35 am, on Wednesday, and inquires, "Do we have a Secretary of State yet?" Hillary Rodham Clinton had not yet been confirmed.

His first meeting on Iraq in the Situation Room got him started. Through his first year in office he continued to work diligently enough to be awarded the Nobel Peace Prize. He had now won the attention of the world and respect of nations.

## THE NOBEL PEACE PRIZE FOR 2009

**The Norwegian Nobel Committee** has decided that the Nobel Peace Prize for 2009 is to be awarded to President Barack Obama for his extraordinary efforts to strengthen international diplomacy and cooperation between peoples. The Committee has attached special importance to Obama's vision of and work for a world without nuclear weapons.

Obama has as President created a new climate in international politics. Multilateral diplomacy has regained a central position, with emphasis on the role that the United Nations and other international institutions can play. Dialogue and negotiations are preferred as instruments for resolving even the most difficult international conflicts. The vision of a world free from nuclear arms has powerfully stimulated disarmament and arms control negotiations. Thanks to Obama's initiative, the USA is now playing a more constructive role in meeting the great climactic challenges the world is confronting. Democracy and human rights are to be strengthened.

Only very rarely has a person to the same extent as Obama captured the world's attention and given its people hope for a better future. His diplomacy is founded in the concept that those who are to lead the world must do so on the basis of values and attitudes that are shared by the majority of the world's population.

For 108 years, the Norwegian Nobel Committee has sought to stimulate precisely that international policy and those attitudes for which Obama is now the world's leading spokesman. The Committee endorses Obama's appeal that "Now is the time for all of us to take our share of responsibility for a global response to global challenges." **ON THE ROAD TO GLORY LAND (PRESIDENT OF USA)**

The most influential woman in the world, OPRAH GAIL WINFREY, endorsed Barack Obama in September 2006, even before he had declared himself a presidential candidate in May 2007. Her Supreme Highness made her first campaign appearance for him, estimating a value of over one million votes in the Democratic primary race. Without this, he most likely would not have won.

"HOME GIRL" (a name we Mississippians call each other) or "HOME BOY" - myself, became intoxicated with the idea that this Black man could lead our country in the right way – with love, grace, and dignity: me, by joining the Democratic Party and making donations and Oprah by having fund raisers. At her California home in the fall of 2007, she raised several million dollars and repeated the gesture in 2008 in Chicago.

Oprah is from Kosciusko, Mississippi. I, Sam Wilson, III, am from Hattiesburg, Mississippi.

After completing his first year as President of the United States of America, he received the Nobel Peace Prize!!!!

# BLOWING YOUR MIND

Alfred Bernard Nobel (/nou'be/) was born in Sweden-Norway in the city of Stockholm in 1833, where his body still lies. He was a chemist, an engineer, an inventor, and a philanthropist-business man. He invented dynamite and was a manufacturer of cannons and other armaments that led to the loss of human lives from which he profited. He became exceedingly wealthy and was criticized for the sales of arms. Feeling guilty, he bequeathed his wealth to establish the NOBEL PRIZE.

The Norwegian Nobel Committee yearly gives in recognition of merit or achievement to the person who shall have done the most or the best work for fraternity between nations, for the abolition or reduction of standing armies, and for the holding and promotion of peace congresses. Those chosen receive a medal, a diploma, and money, along with international honor and glory!

Morehouse College is blessed to have had Dr. Martin Luther King, Jr. as a recipient in 1964. Dr. King at the age of 35 was the youngest person to ever receive the award.

The Norwegian Nobel Committee in 2009 selected President Barack Obama (not then a Morehouse man) on his concept that those who lead the world must do so on the basis of values and attitudes that are shared by the majority of the world's population.

Other White House leaders who share this honor: Theodore Roosevelt in 1906 for his role in ending the Russian-Japanese war; Woodrow Wilson in 1919 for founding the League of Nations; Jimmy Carter in 2002 for human rights, and Vice-President Al Gore in 2007 for his role in climate change.

# HE DON'T PLAY

In the old Western movies, Wild Bill Elliott would say, "I'm a peaceful man" and then pull his pistol and shoot the shit out of his adversary or enemy. So it was with President Obama. Although he sought peace and tranquility, he didn't take any shit. Ask the pirates of Somali, Africa and Osama bin Laden. He could have been irenic, that is favoring, conducive to, or operating toward peace, moderation or conciliation, but he was not!

## THE WELCOMING NEWS OF THE DEATH OF OSAMA BIN LADEN

On May 2, 2011, President Barack Obama said: "Tonight, I can report to the American people and to the world that the United States has conducted an operation that killed Osama bin Laden, the leader of al-Qaeda, and a terrorist who's responsible for the murder of thousands of innocent men, women, and children."

I suppose somebody cried when these words were spoken, perhaps some misguided Muslim on the edge of Damascus, but to me they were liken to a billet-doux, a love letter!

I thought that my hatred for Osama bin Laden was interminable. I simply said, "God bless America. Now I can cease to hate."

And then Obama was not a Morehouse man yet.

## LOVE OF COUNTRY OVER RACE, RELIGION AND DANGERS

When it comes to love for America, things such as race, religion, and heritage should not deter loyal citizens from allegiance to their country. The 442nd Infantry Japanese soldiers fought valiantly for America during World War II. General Dwight D. Eisenhower, who was of German heritage, led and directed the invasion of Germany to end WWII. Barack Obama did not hold back in his duty in ordering the rescue of American cargo ship's captain Richard Phillips from pirates in Mombasa, Kenya (Somalia, Africa), even though he is of African heritage also. He authorized the Navy Seals in the killing of three Somali pirates to facilitate this successful endeavor. Barack Obama was a BAAD Mother F—. He don't Play! Don't mess with him and America!

"I share the country's admiration for the bravery of Captain Phillips and his selfless concern for his crew," Mr. Obama said in a statement. "His courage is a model for all Americans."

### Somalia, Africa

To whom or where should we place the blame of African piracy in the Federal Republic of Somalis? People whom are a mixture of British and/ or Italian with Africans and pure Africans themselves seemed doomed by following the sequence of seeking of wealth by their predecessors who once dominated their lives and government.

Somalia is a country located in the horn of Africa. It borders by Ethiopia on its west, Djibouti on its northeast, the Indian Ocean on its east, the gulf of Aden on its north, and Kenya to the southwest. Somalia has the longest coastline on Africa's mainland.

The majority of its people are Muslims (Sunni). Since the civil war in 1991, their government has been unstable. 43% of the people live on less than 1 U.S. dollar a day. 80% are nomadic. Somalia has the world's largest population of camels.

Its territorial waters are prime fishing grounds for migratory marine species, especially tuna fish. This has caused unwelcomed countries to invade and leave waste, polluting the waters. Somalians retaliated by capturing ships and people, using them as ransom demands. This provided very lucrative dollars, often in the millions.

President Barack Obama said, "No, not our American ships."

# HE GOT GAME

As a former athlete myself, I feel qualified to comment on Obama's athletic abilities. In high school I was a star in basketball and football. At Morehouse College, I played football as a starting tackle, both offense and defense. I also participated in intramural basketball and field events in track.

I've had the privilege of coaching and winning championships in all of the following sports with the exception of two – soccer and wrestling. I have coached:

| | | |
|---|---|---|
| Soccer | Track | Tennis (girls) |
| Wrestling | Volleyball (girls) | Baseball |
| Football | Basketball (both girls and boys) | Softball (girls' fast pitch) |

My room is filled with trophies and awards to substantiate my claim:

I have officiated the following sports:

| | | |
|---|---|---|
| Lacrosse | Basketball | Softball |
| Football | Track | |

while supervising and being a spectator of:

| | |
|---|---|
| Hockey | Gymnastics |
| Swimming | Cheerleading |

How good was he back then? Here's former teammate Mark Bendix in an NBC story.

MOREHOUSE COLLEGE

DEPARTMENT OF PHYSICAL EDUCATION

THIS IS TO CERTIFY THAT

HAS BEEN AWARDED THE

MOREHOUSE VARSITY M IN

FOR THE SEASON OF

ATHLETIC DIRECTOR          COACH

CAPTAIN

S.M.I.C. '86
COACH OF THE YEAR
BOYS BASKETBALL
S. WILSON

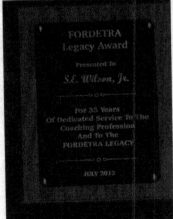

FORDETRA
Legacy Award

Presented To

S.E. Wilson, Jr.

For 35 Years
Of Dedicated Service To The
Coaching Profession
And To The
FORDETRA LEGACY

JULY 2012

# CLARKSTOWN HIGH SCHOOL NORTH COACHING STAFF

LOU TOSCANO
University of Rhode Island 1964
Head Coach

PAUL TOSCANO
University of Wyoming 1968

ANTHONY TETRO
University of Rhode Island 1964
Assistant

TONY PISCITELLI
NORTH
Freshman Coach

SAM WILSON
Morehouse College 1955

FRED BRUNTRAGER
Cortland State Teachers 1972
Freshman Coach

JOHN YUDA
Junior Varsity Coach

# North completes 9-0 season

By STEVE DRUMMOND
Staff Sports Writer

"I guess it really hasn't hit me yet," Clarkstown North Lou Toscano said after Saturday's game against Suffern. What hadn't hit Toscano yet was the PSAL football championship, an unbeaten season, the league's leading defense, a 1,000-yard rusher and as he related a bit later "the happiest day of my life.

All of this was culminated by North's 29-0 triumph over host Suffern. It was a typical Ram win accomplished in a manner now familiar to all North fans. Workmanlike, nothing overly spectacular, solid defense, good running and an occasional pass.

"We wanted to beat everyone. We've heard talk that this team or that team was better than us. Well now we've beat everyone," Toscano said.

"We've been through some lean years, so we've been on both sides of the fence. It's a lot better on this side.

"This was the best group of young men I've had the pleasure of working with. They were seniors, they knew what they had to do and they went out and did it. When these kids were in eighth grade they told me they would win the championship and go unbeaten when they were seniors. Well, they were right."

Clarkstown stopped Suffern cold the first two times the Mounties had possession. The Rams stopped themselves with a fumble after a Tom Sullivan-to-Bruce Fritz completion, but moved for a score on their second possession.

With the Mounties obviously keying on tailback Rick Kolka, fullback Steve Lawson did the bulk of the ball carrying and the bulk of the gaining in the first period. A 15-yard holding penalty stopped the Rams touchdown drive, but a 14-yard completion to Steve Stallone moved the Rams back into field goal range.

The Mounties just did tip John Coulter's attempt from the 27, but Coulter had more than enough foot to make the three-pointer.

Ron Manning's only bad punt of an otherwise good day, set up the winners' next score. North took over at the Mountie 31 and Lawson gained five, Kolka added gains of nine and four and Lawson went the final 13 yards for the score. The latter play was an up-the-middle burst behind fine blocking, with Lawson holding his balance for the final six yards after being tripped up. Coulter's boot was true and the Rams now led 10-0. The rout was on.

North's defense continued to stifle a Suffern offense, playing without their regulars, including top running back Fred Greenberg. Lawson, at defensive end, tackle Dennis Curry and linebackers Chuck Koehler and Tom Dammao were especially outstanding.

Manning later attempted to run from punt formation and almost made it. Almost might help in horseshoes, but in this case it gave the Rams possession at the Mountie 46. Kolka and Sullivan brought it to the 28 with a total of six carries and then Sullivan found Frank Racioppi with a 19-yard strike after rolling right.

Kolka carried the final seven yards, breaking a tackle at the three and moving closer to the 1,000-yard rushing mark. He eventually got that magic figure in the fourth period and wound up the year with 1,011.

(Please turn to 10C)

*Staff photo — Ted Neuhalt*

**Kolka carries**

Clarkstown North halfback Rick Kolka (31) darts through line as finished the season with more than 1,000 yards rushing. North blanked Suffern, 29-0, to finish the season undefeated. In other season-ending PSAL football action Saturday,

Clarkstown South edged Pearl River, 22-21; Tappan Zee rolled Ramapo, 30-7; Nyack walloped Spring Valley, 48-18; and North Rockland beat Nanuet, 14-6. See pages 8C-12C for stories and pictures.

# Rams clinch PSAL grid title

By RICHARD GUTWILLIG
Staff Sports Writer

Clarkstown North, almost on its own, but with a little help for some close friends and neighbors, clinched the 1973 PSAL football championship Saturday with a convincing 22-0 victory over visiting Nyack.

The Rams are now unbeaten in eight games and have a two-game lead over both Suffern and Tappan Zee. Sister school Clarkstown South made next Saturday's Suffern-Clarkstown North contest purely academic as the Vikings dumped Suffern to give North the crown outright.

However, let there be no mistake about it, Clarkstown North under head coach Lou Toscano has done it all this year both offensively and defensively and done it convincingly. And both units made their presence felt Saturday against Nyack.

The offensive squad, led by the running of Rick Kolka and Steve Lawson, and two timely passes from Tom Sullivan to Bruce Fritz, moved for 266 yards. However, the defense was nothing less than tremendous as Nyack gained only eight yards offensively all afternoon. The Indians carried 24 times for minus 32 yards and had four pass completions for 40 yards.

While the statistical battle was all Clarkstown North's, the game itself was an 8-0 squeaker until less than five minutes remained.

Both teams had scouted each other and neither had planned any major offensive changes. Nyack was prepared for the Ram rushing game between the tackles and they saw it. Nyack knew that the Rams would pass occasionally and they did.

North knew that Nyack would depend on the passing of Kenny Gray and had prepared for a hard pass rush with an occasional blitz. Nyack knew it had to try to establish a running attack and it tried, although to no avail.

Thus, with neither team doing anything surprising, it was a matter of which team would do its offensive task better. North did and as a consequence, North won. It was that basic and that simple.

However, the Indians did put up a fierce struggle for most of the game and had nothing to be ashamed of in defeat. North just happens to be a better squad this year primarily because of utilizing 21 seniors and 11 juniors. The Rams have only four sophomores on the varsity squad. Nyack conversely had 29 sophomores and juniors and of that group, 17 saw action Saturday.

Clarkstown kicked off to begin the contest and Nyack moved to one first down on a 23-yard pass from Gray to Robbie Woods. However, the Indians punted and North took over on its 44. Here the pattern was established as the Rams moved on an 11-play march with Kolka and Lawson the only ball carriers. Moving for four first downs, the Ram attack was halted as Nyack staged a fine goal line stand. With a first-and-seven, the Indian defensive unit stopped Kolka and two Lawson runs for a total of five yards.

Pinned deep in its own territory, Nyack punted out to its 38 as the quarter ended. In three plays, North was on the scoreboard with the only points it would need. Kolka was stopped for no gain, then he picked up

(Please turn to 8C)

Clarkstown South Champions

Bendix said, his old pal should have been a starter at Punahou – and insisted he was not just being loyal to an old friend.

"I loved his game," he said. "He had a pretty good shot and really handled the ball well."

And something in that same story on Obama's work ethic from former coach Chris McLachlin:

"He would carry his books in one hand and his ball in the other," he said.

"He lived across the street from school and before classes he'd shoot baskets on the outside courts, then at lunch he'd shoot more baskets, then I'd have him for three hours, then he'd go home, eat supper, and then be outside again shooting baskets."

He then took his game to Occidental College, where former coach Mike Zinn had this to say to the *Los Angeles Times* in 2008:

"He was really athletic, ran good, jumped good," says Zinn, who left coaching about 20 years ago and is a partner in an Orange County sales agency. "He wasn't a great outside shooter. In basketball terminology, he was kind of a slasher. He was left-handed.

He went left well, didn't go right that well.

"He had a nose for the ball, always came up with loose balls and rebounds inside.

So if he got 10 points in a game, most of them were probably under the basket. He didn't hit jump shots from 15 feet or anything like that.

"He was a good defender, definitely a good athlete."

Now, we've established the skills of a young Obama – it sounds like the lefty was your above-average player, one who could perhaps be in a low-level college rotation, but who probably wouldn't start on D-I team.

There isn't much to be found on the president's game between college and his eventual ascension to becoming the junior senator in Illinois in 2005, but there's some video evidence of Obama on the court before he became president.

Obama's famous pickup games over the years were a "who's who" made up of former college players like personal aide Reggie Love (who played at Duke), ex-Illinois treasurer Alexi Giannoulias – a former pro player in Greece – and former Secretary of Education and Harvard co-captain Arne Duncan, who played countless games with Obama over the past few decades.

Duncan spoke to *For The Win* and noted how truly tough and

competitive Obama was on the court. But he also used the word "cerebral" multiple times to describe the president's game:

"He's a fantastic defensive player. He's long, he understands angles, he understands how to force opponents into their weaknesses. Offensively, he's very crafty, very deceptive, will cut back door on you, has a very good crossover dribble.

He'll knock down a shot when he's open.

"I don't say this lightly. He's a great teammate, he's the kind of guy you want on your team because it's all about winning, it's all about doing whatever it takes to win. And that can be big stuff or tiny stuff no one ever notices."

Duncan added Obama is "better going to the basket," but that he can hit open shots from the outside. And when asked if anyone ever took it easy on POTUS, he replied, "Never."

There's also this tidbit he dropped that speaks volumes about Obama both on the court and off it:

"It was not infrequent to see him literally not shoot the ball all game and then would score the final basket or the final two baskets of the game. There are lots of guys who love to get shots up early in games, but when things get a little tight, they'd disappear.

"He was just the opposite. He wanted to take the big shot – he wouldn't force one, wouldn't take a bad one – but after passing and cutting and deferring, all of a sudden he would turn the corner, go to the basket and score, or pump-fake and knock down a shot. "That part says so much about character. When games were close, when things were tough, he wanted the ball in his hands. He lived for those moments."

That group has also expanded occasionally to include celebrities or former pros.

ESPN.com senior writer Andy Katz has played twice with Obama, both on the president's lucky Election Day games. In 2012, that group included Hall of Famer Scottie Pippen.

Katz gave *For The Win* a scouting report this week:

> "He is a solid player for his age. He likes the ball in his hands, is a much better passer than shooter and is much more of a selective shooter. He's not a ball hog and not someone who's going to constantly seek his shot . . .

"He's got quick bursts of speed, I wouldn't say he's the fastest end to end, but he can definitely cut and get to the basket."

Katz added that no one on that day in 2012 said anything about how impressed they were with the president, but "it didn't feel like anyone thought he was the weak link. He held his own."

That phrase turns out ironic. It turns out Obama scaled back on hoops toward the end of his second term and turned more to golf. In 2015, he gave *WTF*'s Marc Maron a state of his game address (via CBS Sports):

"I used to play basketball more but these days I've gotten to the point where it is not as much fun," Obama told Maron. "Because I'm not as good as I used to be and I get frustrated. I was never great but I was a good player and I could play seriously. Now I'm like one of these old guys whose running around.

"The guys I play with who are all a lot younger," Obama continued. "They sort of pity me and sympathize with me. They tolerate me but we all know that I'm the weak link on the court. And I don't like being the weak link."

We'll leave the last word to Obama: He was good, never great. But he played seriously.

# DAMN, HE'S COOL

While campaigning as a senator in July 19, 2008 in the Middle East, Obama met with American forces in Kuwait. There he then demonstrated his skill as a basketball player by draining a three-pointer on his very first try. The troops responded, "Damn, he's cool."

He repeated this gesture by shooting another three-pointer while still wearing his shirt and tie in South Caroline in 2012.

How do you define COOL?

# HE BE CALM AND COLLECTED

July 16, 2009, Louis Gates, a prominent black Harvard professor, returning from a trip to China, could not get into his place of dwelling because of a jammed door. He lived in Cambridge, Massachusetts. Along with his cab driver's help, he succeeded in opening the door. A few minutes later, Police Sgt. James Crowley arrived and requested that Gates step outside. Gates asked why and refused his request – that this was his house, then showed his driver's license and Harvard credentials. Gates then asked the police officer for his name and badge number. Crowley refused and walked to the front porch, turned around, and arrested Gates for disorderly conduct. Crowley said that prior to this he received a call of an attempted burglary in the area. Gates said he was mistreated because he was an African-American.

During a press conference, Obama was asked his opinion. He replied, "I don't know, not having been there and not seeing all the facts what role race played in that. But I think it's fair to say: number one, any of us would be pretty angry; number two, that the Cambridge police acted stupidly in arresting somebody when there was already proof that they were in their own home; and number three, what I think we know separate and apart from this incident is that there's a long history in this country of Afro-Americans and Latinos being stopped by law enforcement disproportionately."

For this he was criticized and seemed to be leaning towards his black heritage rather than his white. He dare not afford this image.

I, the writer, am a beer drinker and have been since my Morehouse College days. Just off campus down the street was a place we called "The Draft Board" where cool, delicious draft beer could be procured. When I had the money or was treated by others, I would enjoy myself there.

On July 24, Obama invited both Crowley and Gates, along with his vice-president Joe Biden, to a beer drinking gathering at the White House, where they resolved their problems amiably. Thus the "Beer Summit." That is when I became acquainted with "Blue Moon" beer. I suppose this increased the sales of the brewer.

# "AIN'T HE GOT GOOD RELIGION? CERTAINLY, CERTAINLY LORD"

*⌒ɱᖺ⌒*

People began to question Barack Obama's religion. Some suggested that he was Muslim, others associated him with Christianity. And if so, what denomination – Catholic, Methodist, Episcopal, Presbyterian, AME, CME? But when I saw him deliver the eulogy in South Carolina for the Reverend Clementa Pinckney and sang *Amazing Grace*, I knew then he was a black "hard shell" Baptist.

Case closed. I wondered if he ate collard greens and fried chicken at the repast?

You know the song, don't you?

## AMAZING GRACE
(written by John Newton and Liam Joseph Hurley)

Amazing grace! How sweet the sound
That saved a wretch like me.
I once was lost, but now am found,
Was blind, but now I see.

'Twas grace that taught my heart to fear,
And grace my fear relieved.
How precious did that grace appeared
The hour I first believed.

Through many dangers, toil and snares
I have already come:
'Tis grace hath brought me safe thus far-reaching
And grace will lead me home.

And please note that Obama was a member of his high school's choir in 1977.

# HE BE COOL AND DETERMINED

I don't know if Obama smoked Kool cigarettes, but he was a cool and determined "Dude."

I think he gave up the smoking habit just as I gave up Lucky Strike cigarettes. He did not, however, give up his quest for assisting the less fortunate Americans by signing The Affordable Care Act 2010. Five of his predecessors for a hundred years failed to create universal health insurance for our country.

As it stands now, over 30 million uninsured Americans shall benefit. Thank you, Guy!

# HE BE A FUNNY MAN

His sense of humor is overwhelming!

If there is any doubt about what Barack Obama should do after leaving the White House, I suggest that he try his hand as a standup comedian. He has a great sense of humor. Here are some of my favorite amusing or biographical incident jokes.

1.  On the productivity of Congress - "I want to especially thank all members of Congress who took a break from their exhausting schedule of not passing laws to be here tonight.

2.  "This is a tough holiday for Rahm Emanuel. He is not used to saying the word DAY after Mother."

3.  On his pot smoking days - "Look, when I was a kid, I inhaled frequently. That was the point."

4.  On his birth certificate challenge - "What a week. As some of you have heard, the state of Hawaii released my official long-form birth certificate. Hopefully, this puts all doubts to rest. But just in case they're any lingering questions, tonight I'm prepared to go a step further. Tonight, for the first, I am releasing my official birth video.

5.  On Trump's reversal - "There is an extra spring in my step tonight. I don't know about you guys, but I am so relieved that the whole birther thing is over. I mean ISIL, North Korea, poverty, climate change, none of those things weighed on my mind like the validity of my birth certificate."

6.  On attacks against him by Republicans - "I've been called worse on the basketball court."

7.  On Republicans - "I know Republicans are still sorting out what happened in 2012, but one thing they all agree on is they need to do a better job reaching out to minorities. And look, call me self-centered, but I can think of one minority they could start with.

8. On his two terms as president - "Actually, I think it's a good idea that I'm limited to serving only two terms. If I ran a third time it'd be like doing a third Hangover movie. Didn't really work out very well, did it?"

9. On poking fun at the press - "The White House Correspondent's Dinner is known as the Prom of Washington D.C. - a term coined by political reporters who clearly never had the chance to go to an actual prom.

10. On love for his Vice-President - "I tease Joe Biden sometimes, but he has been at my side for seven years, I love that man. He is not just a great Vice-President, he is a great friend. We've gotten so close in some places in Indiana, they won't serve us pizza anymore."

(Taken from *The Reader's Digest*)

My spouse, Ruby Jewel, and myself have traveled extensively and have indulged in whatever the area we are visiting is noted for: its history, its geography, its monuments, its food and drinks, and let's not forget, its shopping promenades. We have covered the United States of America with the exception of the state of Oregon. We have eaten gumbo in New Orleans, Louisiana; Maryland crabs in Baltimore; Maine lobsters in Bar Harbor, Maine; dined in some of New York's finest steak restaurants and eaten in its China Town, Little Italy and Jewish Delis. We have traveled to Boston for chowder and scrod; eaten barbecue in Chicago, Memphis, and St. Louis; tasted chili in Montana; and fried chicken, catfish, and grits in Mississippi. We have tasted mussels in Brussels; pizza in Italy; fish and chips in London; french onion soup in Paris; and dined at the Brown Derby in California. We have drank beer in Germany and wine in France, Italy, and Spain.

I have many friends that are of Italian heritage, so naturally I have eaten with them, either in their places of dwelling or their favorite restaurants. (You should see them at my house eating collard greens, cornbread, ham hocks, and fried chicken!) Everybody in New York, regardless of their heritage, seems to boast of their favorite Italian restaurant. I, too, have my favorite Italian eatery, Fellini's, introduced to me by my non-Italian, but native New Yorker friend, Clifton Hall. Our next door neighbor and close friend, Anthony Ripolone, now of Yonkers, New York, not only served us savory food from his grill and kitchen but also treated us to food at his favorite restaurant in "Little Italy," New York – Luna's.

*Mangia bene, Ridi spesso, Ama molto*

I would be amiss, when referring to outstanding Italian cuisine not to mention the names of:

**Marie and Anthony Mancuso**
**Patricia and Anthony Tetro**
**Rose and Lenny Frisaro**
**Kathy and Ralph Femiani**

I do not know who is the best, and even if I did, I would not say so!!

After experiencing all of these, then why am I so enthused about what the President and past Presidents of America eat or ate, drink or drank? I don't know, just curious that's all. So I'll share it with you. Now let me pervade your mind, also.

# FOODS THAT BARACK OBAMA EATS

Breakfast is the most important meal of the day. A simple bowl of cereal in the morning may curb a tendency toward obesity and late-night cravings, boost metabolism, and lower cholesterol levels, but eating breakfast also benefits the brain.

Studies show that a morning meal enhances memory and cognitive function. Barack Obama usually eats four to six eggs, potatoes, and wheat toast, and every now and then fruit, bacon and oatmeal.

## PRESIDENT OBAMA'S FAVORITE MEALS

President Barack Obama is skinny, as he often describes himself. He's actually lost weight on the campaign trail. He is a comfort-food guy and his favorite grub is a steaming bowl of chili. His wife, Michelle, said that while cooking for Obama, she'd put a low-calorie, high-fiber spin on this classic dish and make him a rib-sticking bowl of Beef and Bean Chile Verde served with all the fixings – reduced-fat sour cream, grated cheddar cheese, chopped scallions and chopped fresh tomatoes. Other foods that Obama has been known to enjoy are shrimp and grits.

His favorite restaurant is Italian Fiesta Pizzeria and Rick Bayless' Topolobampo, a high-end homage to regional Mexican cooking in Chicago. His family has hankerings for Mexican food, enjoys hand-crafted pastas and his kids dig fried chicken and macaroni and cheese.

During a walking tour of the Italian market, Obama ate salami with baked ricotta that he compared to pound cake, provolone and mozzarella. Actually when it comes to food, Obama eats pretty much anything, from chicken wings and barbecue and ribs to grilled fish and steamed broccoli. But when he is campaigning in a small town with limited options, a cheeseburger is always a good bet (Cheddar is the cheese of choice). Obama likes MET-Rx chocolate roasted-peanut protein bars and bottles of a hard-to-find organic brew – Black Forest Berry Honest Tea. He keeps a supply of both on hand.

Obama savors the following foods:

>Planters trail mix: nuts, seeds and raisins
>Roasted almonds
>Pistachios
>Water
>Dentyne ice
>Nicorette
>MET-Rx chocolate roasted peanut protein bars
>Vegetables, especially broccoli and spinach
>Handmade milk chocolates from Fran's chocolates in Seattle

Obama dislikes the following food:

>Mayonnaise
>Salt and vinegar potato chips
>Asparagus ("if no other vegetables are available, he'll eat it")
>Beets
>Soft drinks (he prefers water)
>Ice cream

Obama's family chili

Obama has been using this chili recipe since college. Obama's family chili recipe is as follows:

1 large onion, chopped
1 green pepper, chopped
Several cloves of garlic, chopped
1 tablespoon olive oil
1 pound ground turkey or beef
¼ teaspoon ground cumin
¼ teaspoon ground oregano
¼ teaspoon ground turmeric
¼ teaspoon ground basil
1 tablespoon chili powder
3 tablespoons red wine vinegar
Several tomatoes, depending on size, chopped
1 can red kidney beans

Saute onion, green pepper, and garlic in olive oil until soft. Add ground meat and brown. Combine spices together into a mixture, then add to ground meat. Add red wine vinegar. Add tomatoes and let simmer, until tomatoes cook down. Add kidney beans and cook for a few more minutes. Serve over white or brown rice. Garnish with grated cheddar cheese, onions and sour cream.

# DRINKING AND EATING HABITS OF UNITED STATES PRESIDENTS

*ℳ*

All of our Presidents had their unique and preferable styles of consuming food and alcohol. Perhaps it is due to their childhood upbringing, location, time, and environment. Check these out if you care:

| PRESIDENT | FOOD | DRINK |
|---|---|---|
| 1. George Washington | Cherries | Dark Porter |
| 2. John Adams | Apple pan dowdy | Porter beer, rum & Maderia |
| 3. Thomas Jefferson | Virginia sweet corn | Wine |
| 4. James Madison | Virginia ham | Champagne |
| 5. James Monroe | Chicken fried with rice | Burgundy champagne -French |
| 6. John Quincy Adams | Fresh fruits | Maderia wine |
| 7. Andrew Jackson | Leather britches, green beans, bacon and duck | Whiskey |
| 8. Martin Van Buren | Boar's head | Whiskey |
| 9. William Harrison | Hard cider | Same |

| | | |
|---|---|---|
| 10. John Tyler | Grateful pudding | Champagne |
| 11. James Polk | Corn pone | Champagne-wine-brandy |
| 12. Zachary Taylor | Calas-tous-chauds | Whiskey |
| 13. Millard Fillmore | Beef stew | Rarely drank |
| 14. Franklin Pierce | New Hampshire fried pie | Drunkest President ever |
| 15. James Buchanan | Moss Rose cake | Maderia; sherry |
| 16. Abraham Lincoln | Honey | Not really a drinker |
| 17. Andrew Johnson | Sweet potato | Whiskey |
| 18. Ulysses Grant | Rice pudding | Treated his guests with the highest champagne |
| 19. Rutherford Hayes | Angel cake | Rum |
| 20. James Garfield | Squirrel soup | Beer (not much) |
| 21. Chester A. Arthur | Macaroni pie with oysters | "Alcohol is the devil" |
| 22. Grover Cleveland | Corn beef and cabbage | |
| 23. Benjamin Harrison | Fig pudding | Beer – lots of it |
| 24. Grover Cleveland | | |

| | | |
|---|---|---|
| 25. William McKinley | Lobster salad | McKinley's Delight -drink named after him |
| 26. Theodore Roosevelt | Coffee | Mint Julep |
| 27. William H. Taft | Steak | Champagne (occasionally) |
| 28. Woodrow Wilson | Strawberry ice cream | Scotch |
| 29. Warren G. Harding | Chicken pot pie | Whiskey |
| 30. Calvin Coolidge | Corn muffins | Tokay wine |
| 31. Herbert Hoover | Egg timbales | Dry martini |
| 32. Franklin Roosevelt | White fish | Cocktails |
| 33. Harry Truman | Fried chicken | Bourbon |
| 34. Dwight D. Eisenhower | Beef stew | Light drinker (heart problems) |
| 35. John F. Kennedy | New England fish chowder | Scotch and a lot different others |
| 36. Lyndon B. Johnson | Texas barbecue | Scotch |
| 37. Richard Nixon | Cottage cheese | Expensive Chateau Lafite |
| 38. Gerald Ford | Crab soup and honey made bread | Martinis |

| | | |
|---|---|---|
| 39. Jimmy Carter | Baked grits/cheese | Small glass of white wine |
| 40. Ronald Reagan | Honey baked apples | California wine |
| 41. George H. W. Bush | Corn pudding | Everything |
| 42. Bill Clinton | Chicken enchiladas | Snakebite (cider and beer) |
| 43. George W. Bush | Huevo rancheros | Quit drinking |
| 44. Barack Obama | Black Forest Berry | Beer Honest Tea |

# TWO PLACES OF GRANDEUR

I have a nephew, Percy Howard, a Jackson State (Mississippi) graduate who is a Secret Service Agent and who has traveled all over the world protecting President Obama. There are two places he did not go with him (what a shame!): Jordan's lost city of Petra and Martha's Vineyard.

On March 23, 2013, President Barack Obama, ending his Middle East tour, took a visit to Petra to tour the treasured city. After seeing these wonderful structures, he marveled and said, "This is pretty spectacular. It's amazing."

During this trip, Prime Minister Benjamin Netanyahu apologized to Turkey for a 2010 commando raid that killed nine activists on a Turkish vessel in Gaza Bound Flotilla. This apology was welcomed by Prime Minister Recep Erdogan of Turkey and eased the hostile feelings between Israel and Turkey, now allies in the Middle East.

The Obamas vacationed in Martha's Vineyard, Massachusetts, a beautiful off-shore island off Cape Cod. It is an affluent pleasure spot for moguls, movie stars, professional athletes, etc. The Obamas, along with their dogs, are just a part of the scenery. They are not the first White House vacationers; Bill and Hilary Clinton have vacationed there. So did Ulysses S. Grant in 1874. Barack, Michelle, Malia, Sasha, and their dogs Bo and Sunny, lived in a rental called BLUE HERON FARM!

There is a Morehouse school mate, George White of Knoxville, Tennessee (from Birmingham, Alabama) who has a vacation house in Martha's Vineyard. I wonder – did he and his family associate with the Obamas?

Petra

# PETRA

They seem no work of man's created hand,
Where labour wrought as wayward fancy planned;
But from the rock as if by magic grown,
Eternal – silent – beautiful – alone!

Not virgin – white – like that old Doric shrine
Where once Athena held her rites divine.
Not saint grey – like many a minister fane
That crowns the hill, or sanctifies the plain.

John William Burgon

# PATRIARCH-PATERNITY

## HE BE A GOOD FATHER

Sigmund Freud said, "I cannot not think of any need in childhood as strong as the need for a father's protection."

Barack Obama did not grow up with a father at home. Instead he was only two years old when his father abandoned he and his mother to return to Africa. But in spite of this, he became a great man and a devoted father.

Here is a list of some great people that overcame fatherless adversities and succeeded:

Charlie Chaplin

John Lennon, who lost his father three months before his birth

President Bill Clinton, whose father died in an automobile accident (William Jefferson "Bill" Blythe, Jr.). His mother remarried Roger Clinton.

George Washington, who was only 10 years old when his father died

Thomas Jefferson was 14 when his father died

Confucius, Plato, Aristotle, and Genghis Kahn all grew up without fathers.

Julius Caesar was 15 when his father died

General Robert E. Lee was 11 years old when his father abandoned them

Michael Phelps, the greatest swimmer ever, was only 7 when his father abandoned them

Lance Armstrong, the biker, was only 2 years old when his father abandoned them

LeBron James(King James), the basketball player's, father (an ex-con), abandoned he and his 16 year old mother

My grandfather, Samuel Earl Wilson I, abandoned my grandmother Lula and her three sons, all of whom became great fathers themselves

According to Barack Obama.net:

> By all accounts Barack Obama is a great father and a great husband. And it is wonderful to see such a fine man, who is grounded in his family, ascending to the presidency.

> You see, Barack Obama has his priorities in order: he works diligently as a politician, but always ensures that there is adequate quality time for his children and wife.

> So, Barack Obama is not only an intelligent man, a great politician, a great leader and a great American; but he is also a great family man.

## JUST A FEW MORE FATHERLESS GREATS

Kevin Durant

Shaquille O'Neal

Alex Rodriquez

Ray Lewis

Larry Bird (father committed suicide)

Jackie Robertson

Colin Kaepernick

Sir Issac Newton, born on Christmas Day, December 25, 2642. Father also named Isaac Newton died three months before his birth.

# FAMILY MAN

# 8 YEARS OF GLORY

BROTHERS AND SISTAS (Siblings) There are two extremes in my family heritage; One, There were only five of us, my mother, my father, myself and my twin sisters. My mother's family consisted of five members also, She and two younger brothers, while my father's family consisted of two younger brothers, a father and a mother. By Black folks standards these are small, whereas my mother's father came from a family of 11 which produced one sister that gave birth to 25 children and another who produced 29.

After seeing photographs of Barack Obama, his beautiful wife and children and his pure bred dogs, one would assume that that was all of his family to see. Quite the contrary!

Barack had eight (8), Siblings by four other marriages and/or indulgences by both of his parents.

1.  A half-sister, Maya Soetoro, from his mother's second marriage, born in Indonesia who lives in Hawaii.
2.  From Obama's father's first and third marriages in Africa, half-brother Malik Obama and half-sister, Auma Obama. Also Mark Ndesandjo and David Nedsandjo.
3.  An illegitimate half-brother, George Hussein Obama
4.  Half-brothers, adopted, Abo Obama and Bernard Obama

I think that the closest bond with Barack is Maya Soetoro, although he seems to care for them all...

# AMERICA IS BEAUTIFUL, BUT

When President Barack Obama presided over America, he most likely was influenced by these words by Katherine Lee Bates:

O beautiful for spacious skies,
For amber waves of grain,
For purple mountain majesties
Above the fruited plain!
America! America!
God shed his grace on thee
And crown thy good with brotherhood
From sea to shining sea!

And these by Irving Berlin:

God Bless America,
Land that I love.
Stand beside her, and guide her
Thru the night with a light from above.
From the mountains, to the prairies,
To the oceans, white with foam
God bless America, my home sweet home.

America is all of this and more, the greatest country on planet earth. But it also is a land filled with lachrymose episodes, egregious events, and evil people.

During Obama's administration, he must have shed a thousand tears over 14 mass shootings, where he delivered 14 speeches with sorrow and eloquence. These horrific events

1. The first Fort Hood shooting       November 5, 2009

2. The Tucson Congressional event       January 8, 2011

3. Aurora Movie Theater       July 20, 2012

4. The Wisconsin Sikh Temple       August 6, 2012

5. The Sandy Hook Elementary School shooting       December 14, 2012

6. The Navy yard shooting       September 16, 2013

7. The second Fort Hood shooting       April 12, 2014

8. Kansas Jewish Community Center       April 14, 2014

9. The Charleston Church murders       June 18, 2015

10. The Chattanooga Recruiting Center       July 16, 2015

11. Rosenburg Community College       October 1, 2015

12. The San Bernadino Community Center       December 2, 2015

13. Kalamazoo Uber Driver shooting       February 22, 2016

14. The Orlando Nightclub shooting       June 12, 2016

God Bless America – God Bless Obama!

# IN TIMES OF DISASTER

"He be an anchor when it rained"

"Oh, Noah got mad cause de rain kept droppin, Didn't it rain forty days, forty nights without stopping?"

"In times like these you need a Savior. In times like these you need an Anchor. My anchor holds and grips the Solid Rock."

During Obama's presidency, he experienced 81 calamities in 2010, 89 in 2011, and 81 in 2012. In 2011, there were 24 emergencies and 66 major disasters. Admix these catastrophic contingencies, he stood taller than the Empire State building, the Washington monument, and the Lincoln Memorial. The president used every legal device, disposal, FEMA included, making certain that funds were availed where needed.

Even in man-made disasters, like the oil spill in the Gulf of Mexico, he visited Gulfport, in my state of Mississippi on a two-day tour of Mississippi, Alabama, and Florida, making sure that the money paid by the oil company was escrowed fairly. President Obama acknowledged the toll of the massive spill.

We can still enjoy the savor of our shrimps, crabs, fish, and oysters along the beautiful cities of the Mississippi Gulf Coast (Biloxi, Pass Christian, Gulfport, and many more). Thank you, Barack Obama!

# ABOUT THE SONGS

**Didn't It Rain or Oh, Didn't It Rain:**

This is an American gospel song or spiritual song or work song that appeared in sheet music for piano art song form in 1919, arranged by Henry Thacker Burleigh.

## DIDN'T IT RAIN
(written by Harry Bluestone)

Didn't it rain, children
Talk 'bout rain, oh, my Lord
Didn't it, didn't it, didn't it oh my Lord

Didn't it rain?

# IN TIMES LIKE THESE

During the fearful days at the height of World War II, this comforting hymn was written.

In the midst of a busy day as a housewife, Ruth Caye Jones felt a direct inspiration from a Holy Spirit. She stopped her work to quickly put down both words and music, just as they were given to her by God.

Since that day the hymn has been a blessing to countless Christians at special times of need. It has brought comfort during illness, has been used widely at funerals, has encouraged and challenged Christian workers, and drawn many to salvation.

Mrs. Jones experienced for herself the consolation the words of the song could bring as she spent time recovering from serious surgery a few years after it was written.

In times like these, you need a Savior,
In times like these, you need an anchor;
Be very sure, be very sure,
Your anchor holds and grips the Solid Rock!

CHORUS:

The Rock is Jesus, Yes, He's the One,
The Rock is Jesus, The only One
Be very sure, be very sure, Your anchor holds,
And grips the Solid Rock

# U.S. AUTOMOBILE INDUSTRY SAVED

Thank you, President Obama, for giving me the privilege to drive the beautiful convertible Chevrolet, the Cadillac CTS, and the Chrysler Imperial, plus Fords that didn't use the money loans made available by you through banks. Some of America's car industries were facing financial ruins and threats of going under, shutting down. Obama saved the domestic auto industry in 2009, thereby also saving an industry that employs 2.1 million Americans directly and another 2 million jobs in other sections supported auto industry employment. "SEE THE USA IN YOUR CHEVROLET!"

Also, by you and Raul Castro reversing 60 years of tension between American and Cuba – by restoring diplomatic ties we can now visit Cuba and buy our cigars there instead of Jamaica!

# SCIENCE, MEDICINE, TECHNOLOGY

I, Sam Wilson, the writer, am a retired high school science teacher. For forty years I taught high school science, both physical and biological. Naturally, I supported a president who was pro-scientific.

April 29, 2013, President Obama reiterated his strong support for science and technology to members of THE NATIONAL ACADEMY OF SCIENCE at its 150th annual meeting. This organization was founded by President Abraham Lincoln during the Civil War.

President Obama had this to say: "Science, technology, engineering and medicine are critical to the nation's prosperity. Noting that investments made today are bound to pay off for many years to come."

He was concerned that climate change is occurring and is likely caused by the emission of greenhouse gases from human activities.

President Obama also encouraged our youths to engage more enthusiastically in mathematics, physics, chemistry, and technology – to pursue and compete in science fairs.

On stem cell research, while advocating it, he had this to say: "Rather than furthering discovery, our government has forced what I believe is a false choice between sound science and moral value. In this case, I believe the two are not inconsistent. As a person of faith, I believe we are called to care for each other and work to ease human suffering. I believe we have been given the capacity and will to pursue this research and the humanity and conscience to do so responsibly."

# THE PRECISION MEDICINE INITIATIVE

## So What Is Precision Medicine?

It's health care tailored to you. In his 2015 State of the Union address, President Obama announced that he was launching the Precision Medicine initiative – a bold new research effort to revolutionize how we improve health and treat disease and keeps our families healthier.

Advances in Precision Medicine have already led to powerful new discoveries and several new treatments that are tailored to specific characteristics, such as a person's genetic makeup, or the genetic profile of an individual's tumor. This is helping transform the way we can treat diseases such as cancer: Patients with breast, lung, and colorectal cancers, as well as melanomas and leukemias, for instance, routinely undergo molecular testing as part of patient care, enabling physicians to select treatments that improve chances of survival and reduce exposure to adverse effects.

And we're committed to protecting your privacy every step of the way. The White House is working with the Department of Health and Human Services and other federal agencies to solicit input from patient groups, bioethicists, privacy and civil liberties advocates, technologists, and other experts, to help identify and address any legal and technical issues related to the privacy and security of data in the context of Precision Medicine.

The future of precision medicine will enable health care providers to tailor treatment and prevention strategies to people's unique characteristics, including their genome sequence, microbiome composition, health history, lifestyle, and diet. To get there, we need to incorporate many different types of data, from metabolomics (the chemicals in the body at a certain point in time), the microbiome (the collection of microorganisms in or on the body), and data about the patient collected by health care providers and the patients themselves. Success will require that health data is portable, that it can be easily shared between providers, researchers, and most importantly, patients and research participants.

Agencies across the Federal government are doing important work to support the President's vision. This is an "all of government" effort, leveraging the unique expertise and history of each agency to carry forward the President's vision of individualized treatments for every American. Here's how each participating agency is moving ahead to implement PMI:

- Department of Health and Human Services (HHS)
- Department of Veterans Affairs
- Department of Defense

# PRESIDENT OBAMA VISITS ATLANTA

President Barack Obama smiles as Dr. Willis Sheftall performs the honorary degree ceremony during Morehouse College's spring commencement on May 19, 2013, in Atlanta. Ten thousand guests and more than 500 graduates witnessed this empyreal tapestry of the universe.

And now President Obama qualifies to embrace the mystique that surrounds all Morehouse men . . . making them stand apart from others and draws admiration that signifies accomplishments in jobs well done!

If you do not know what I mean – I quote myself, taken from my book *MEMOIRS OF A MOREHOUSE MAN*.

## THE MYSTIQUE?

What is it? Just what is it about this place – these hallowed grounds that blend brotherhood and friendship, that compel us to achieve better than others, that bind one brother to another with a twine so strong that not even death can untangle or break it?

When one of us dies, we cite

*If tears could build a stairway and memories a lane,*
*We'd walk right up to heaven and bring you home again.*
*Back home to again to dear old Morehouse.*

No matter who we are or where we are from – from Manhattan to Memphis - from the San Francisco bay to the bay of Mobile – from Alaska to Atlanta – from Jackson Hole, Wyoming to the swimming hole where I swam in Hattiesburg, Mississippi – from Macon, Georgia to Miami, Florida – from the Green Mountains of Vermont to the White Mountains of New Hampshire to the Tetons of Wyoming and the Great Smoky Mountains of North Carolina – our spirit binds and brotherhood sings loudly, "We shall ever, yea forever, give ourselves in loyalty."

Greek fraternities take a back seat to the fraternal love of Morehouse. Alphas, Kappas, Sigmas, Omegas, and non-Greeks all join hands and sing together - "Morehouse College, Bless Her Name" and "Dear Old Morehouse"!

I have seen so many of my Morehouse friends die, and I wonder, "Why them instead of me? Why am I still here?" I believe I know the answer. I am blessed to live so that I may tell the stories of those beloved heroes who have departed without due recognition.

Let the words resound that these men of Morehouse, known only in the communities that they served, have left indelible and noble marks on mankind and have raised the standards of the world. Their deeds have not been televised, nor have their works of art been proclaimed internationally, but hundreds of us who benefited are living testimonies of their worth and merit.

As William Cullen Bryant asks in his poem *Thanatopsis*, ". . . and what if thou withdraw in silence from the living, and no friend take note of their departure?"

Morehouse College, bless the names of:

| | |
|---|---|
| Samuel E. Wilson – | my father, an educator; The book *One Hundred Miles from New Orleans* – his biography; |
| Clifton Hall – | my friend and lawyer; |
| Ratio Jones – | chemistry teacher, Alcorn State University; |
| Charles Hubert – | acting president, Jackson College, Jackson, Mississippi; |
| B. Baldwin Dansby – | president, Jackson College, Jackson, Mississippi; |
| Tellis B. Ellis – | athletic director, Jackson State University, Jackson, Mississippi |
| Richard Demas – | friend and coach |

# AND WE'LL EVER YEA FOREVER
# GIVE OURSELVES IN LOYALTY

Thanks to the brilliant president of Morehouse College, DR. JOHN SILVANUS WILSON, JR., Barack Obama became a Morehouse Man. And I cried, "All is well, all is well."

At Morehouse College's 129th Commencement, President Barack Obama delivered the commencement address and was given an honorary degree. HALLELUJAH!

## WHY MOREHOUSE?
### May 2013

At its 129th Commencement in May, Morehouse President John Silvanus Wilson, Jr. ('79) announced February 16.

A White House official told the *Atlanta Journal Constitution* that Morehouse was chosen because it is one of the nation's leading historically black colleges and universities and is among the best and brightest institutions of higher education in the country. The official also said that Morehouse is known for its high standard for excellence in learning and social consciousness and is home to a long list of notable alumni that spans the last three centuries.

With this, I conclude my story. I rest my case!

Samuel Earl Wilson, III
Class of 1955

# PRESIDENT OBAMA DELIVERS MOREHOUSE COLLEGE COMMENCEMENT ADDRESS

## JUNE 2, 2016

I have to say that it is one of the great honors of my life to be able to address this gathering here today. I want to thank Dr. Wilson for his outstanding leadership, and the Board of Trustees. We have Congressman Cedric Richmond and Sanford Bishop – both proud alumni of this school, as well as Congressman Hank Johnson. And one of my dear friends and a great inspiration to us all – the great John Lewis is here. We have your outstanding Mayor, Mr. Kasim Reed, in the house.

To all the members of the Morehouse family. And most of all, congratulations to this distinguished group of Morehouse Men – the Class of 2013.

I have to say that it's a little hard to follow – not Dr. Wilson, but a skinny guy with a funny name. Betsegaw Tadele – he's going to be doing something.

I also have to say that you all are going to get wet. And I'd be out there with you if I could. But Secret Service gets nervous. So I'm going to have to stay here, dry. But know that I'm there with you in spirit.

Some of you are graduating summa cum laude. Some of you are graduating magna cum laude. I know some of you are just graduating, "thank you, Lordy." That's appropriate because it's a Sunday.

I see some moms and grandmas here, aunts, in their Sunday best – although they are upset about their hair getting messed up. Michelle would not be sitting in the rain. She has taught me about hair.

I want to congratulate all of you – the parents, the grandparents, the brothers and sisters, the family and friends who supported these young men in so many ways. This is your day, as well. Just thing about it – your sons, your brothers, your nephews – they spent the last four years far from home and close to Spelman, and yet they are still here today. So you've done something right. Graduates, give a big round of applause to your family for everything that they've done for you.

I know that some of you had to wait in long lines to get into today's ceremony. And I would apologize, but it did not have anything to do with security. Those graduates just wanted you to know what it's like to register for classes here. And this time of year brings a different kind of stress – every senior stopping by Gloster Hall over the past week making sure your name was actually on the list of students who met all the graduation requirements. If it wasn't on the list, you had to figure out why. Was it that library book you lent to that trifling roommate who didn't return it? Was it Dr. Johnson's policy class? Did you get enough Crown Forum credits? On that last point, I'm going to exercise my power as President to declare this speech sufficient Crown Forum credits for any otherwise eligible student to graduate. That is my graduation gift to you. You have a special dispensation.

Now, graduates, I am humbled to stand here with all of you as an honorary Morehouse Man. I finally made it. And as I do, I'm mindful of an old saying: "You can always tell a Morehouse Man—but you can't tell him much." And that makes my task a little more difficult, I suppose. But I think it also reflects the sense of pride that's always been part of this school's tradition.

Benjamin Mays, who served as the president of Morehouse for almost 30 years, understood that tradition better than anybody. He said—and I quote— "It will not be sufficient for Morehouse College, for any college, for that matter, to produce clever graduates . . . but rather honest men, men who can be trusted in public and private life – men who are sensitive to the wrongs, the sufferings, and the injustices of society and who are willing to accept responsibility for correcting [those] ills."

It was that mission—not just to educate men, but to cultivate good men, strong men, upright men—that brought community leaders together just two years after the end of the Civil War. They assembled a list of 37 men, free blacks and freed slaves, who would make up the first prospective class of what later became Morehouse College. Most of those first students had a desire to become teachers and preachers—to better themselves so they could help others do the same.

A century and a half later, times have changed. But the "Morehouse Mystique" still endures. Some of you probably came here from communities where everybody looked like you. Others may have come here in search of a community. And I suspect that some of you probably felt a little bit of culture shock the first time you came together as a class in King's Chapel. All of a sudden, you weren't the only high school sports captain, you weren't the only student council president. You were suddenly in a group of high achievers, and that meant you were expected to do something more.

That's the unique sense of purpose that this place has always infused—the conviction that this is a training ground not only for individual success, but for leadership that can change the world. Dr. King was just 15 years old when he enrolled here at Morehouse. He was an unknown, undersized, unassuming young freshman who lived at home with his parents. And I think it's fair to say he wasn't the coolest kid on campus—for the suits he wore, his classmates called him "Tweed." But his education at Morehouse helped to forge the intellect, the discipline, the compassion, the soul force that would transform America. It was here that he was introduced to the writings of Gandhi and Thoreau, and the theory of civil disobedience. It was here that professors encouraged him to look past the world as it was and fight for the world as it should be. And it was here, at Morehouse, as Dr. King wrote, where "I realized that nobody . . . was afraid."

Not even of some bad weather. I added on that part. I know it's wet out there. But Dr. Wilson told me you all had a choice and decided to do it out here anyway. That's a Morehouse Man talking.

Now, think about it. For black men in the '40s and the '50s, the threat of violence, the constant humiliations, large and small, the uncertainty that you could support a family, the gnawing doubts born of the Jim Crow culture that told you every day that somehow you were inferior, the temptation to shrink from the world, to accept your place, to avoid risks, to be afraid—that temptation was necessarily strong.

And yet, here, under the tutelage of men like Dr. Mays, young Martin learned to be unafraid. And he, in turn, taught others to be unafraid. And over time, he taught a nation to be unafraid. And over the last 50 years, thanks to the moral force of Dr. King and a Moses generation that overcame their fear and their cynicism and their despair, barriers have come tumbling down, and new doors of opportunity have swung open, and laws and hearts and minds have been changed to the point where someone who looks like you can somehow come to serve as President of these United States of America.

So the history we share should give you hope. The future we share should give you hope. You're graduating into an improving job market. You're living in a time when advances in technology and communication put the world at your fingertips. Your generation is uniquely poised for success unlike any generation of African Americans that came before it.

But that doesn't mean we don't have work – because if we're honest with ourselves, we know that too few of our brothers have the opportunities that you've had here at Morehouse. In troubled neighborhoods all across this country—many of them heavily African American—too few of our citizens have role models to guide them. Communities just a couple miles from my house in Chicago, communities just a couple miles from here—they're places where jobs are still too scarce and wages are still too low; where schools are underfunded and violence is pervasive; where too many of our men spend their youth not behind a desk in a classroom, but hanging out on the streets or brooding behind a jail cell.

My job, as President, is to advocate for policies that generate more opportunity for everybody—policies that strengthen the middle class and give more people the chance to climb their way into the middle class. Policies that create more good jobs and reduce poverty, and educate more children, and give more families the security of health care, and protect more of our children from the horrors of gun violence. That's my job. Those are matters of public policy, and it is important for all of us—black, white and brown—to advocate for an America where everybody has got a fair shot in life. Not just some. Not just a few.

But along with collective responsibilities, we have individual responsibilities. There are some things, as black men, we can only do for ourselves. There are some things, as Morehouse Men, that you are obliged to do for those still left behind. As Morehouse Men, you now wield something even more powerful than the diploma you're about to collect—and that's the power of your example.

So what I ask of you today is the same thing I ask of every graduating class I address: Use that power for something larger than yourself. Live up to President Mays's challenge. Be "sensitive to the wrongs, the sufferings, and the injustices of society." And be "willing to accept responsibility for correcting [those] ills."

I know that some of you came to Morehouse from communities where life was about keeping your head down and looking out for yourself. Maybe you feel like you escaped, and now you can take your degree and get that fancy job and the nice house and the nice car—and never look back. And don't get me wrong—with all those student loans you've had to take out, I know you've got to earn some money. With doors open to you that your parents and grandparents could not even imagine, no one expects you to take a vow of poverty. But I will say it betrays a poverty of ambition if all you think about is what goods you can buy instead of what good you can do.

So, yes, go get that law degree. But if you do, ask yourself if the only option is to defend the rich and powerful, or if you can also find the time to defend the powerless. Sure, go get your MBA, or start that business. We need black businesses out there. But ask yourselves what broader purpose your business might serve, in putting people to work, or transforming a neighborhood. The most successful CEOs I know didn't start out intent just on making money —rather, they had a vision of how their product or service would change things, and the money followed.

Some of you may be headed to medical school to become doctors. But make sure you heal folks in underserved communities who really need it, too. For generations, certain groups in this country—especially African Americans—have been desperate in need of access to quality, affordable health care. And as a society, we're finally beginning to change that. Those of you who are under the age of 26 already have the option to stay on your parent's health care plan. But all of you are heading into an economy where many young people expect not only to have multiple jobs, but multiple careers.

So starting October 1st, because of the Affordable Care Act—otherwise known as Obamacare—you'll be able to shop for a quality, affordable plan that's yours and travels with you—a plan that will insure not only your health, but your dreams if you are sick or get in an accident. But we're going to need some doctors to make sure it works, too. We've got to make sure everybody has good health in this country. It's not just good for you, it's good for this country. So you're going to have to spread the word to your fellow young people. Which brings me to a second point: Just as Morehouse has taught you to expect more of yourselves, inspire those who look up to you to expect more of themselves. And I have to say, growing up, I made quite a few myself. Sometimes I wrote off my own failings as just another example of the world trying to keep a black man down. I had a tendency sometimes to make excuses for me not doing the right thing. But one of the things that all of you have learned over the last four years is there's no longer any room for excuses.

I understand there's a common fraternity creed here at Morehouse: "Excuses are tools of the incompetent used to build bridges to nowhere and monuments of nothingness." Well, we've got no time for excuses. Not because the bitter legacy of slavery and segregation have vanished entirely; they have not. Not because racism and discrimination no longer exist; we know those are still out there. It's just that in today's hyperconnected, hypercompetitive world, with millions of young people from China and India and Brazil—many of whom started with a whole lot less than all of you did—all of them entering the global workforce alongside you, nobody is going to give you anything that you have not earned.

Nobody cares how tough your upbringing was. Nobody cares if you suffered some discrimination. And moreover, you have to remember that whatever you've gone through, it pales in comparison to the hardships previous generations endured—and they overcame them. And if they overcame them, you can overcome them, too.

You now hail from a lineage and legacy of immeasurably strong men— men who bore tremendous burdens and still laid the stones for the path on which we now walk. You wear the mantle of Frederick Douglass and Booker T. Washington, and Ralph Bunche and Langston Hughes, and George Washington Carver and Ralph Abernathy and Thurgood Marshall, and, yes Dr. Martin Luther King, Jr. These men were many things to many people. And they knew full well the role that racism played in their lives. But when it came to their own accomplishments and sense of purpose, they had no time for excuses.

Every one of you have a grandma or an uncle or a parent who's told you that at some point in life, as an African American, you have to work twice as hard as anyone else if you want to get by. I think President Mays put it even better: He said, "Whatever you do, strive to do it so well that no man living and no man dead, and no man yet to be born can do it any better."

And I promise you, what was needed in Dr. Mays's time, that spirit of excellence, and hard work, and dedication, and no excuses is needed now more than ever. If you think you can just get over in this economy just because you have a Morehouse degree, you're in for a rude awakening. But if you stay hungry, if you keep hustling, if you keep on your grind and get other folks to do the same—nobody can stop you.

And when I talk about pursuing excellence and setting an example, I'm not just talking about in your professional life. One of today's graduates, Frederick Anderson—where's Frederick? Frederick, right here. I know it's raining, but I'm going to tell about Frederick. Frederick started his college career in Ohio, only to find out that his high school sweetheart back in Georgia was pregnant. So he came back and enrolled in Morehouse to be closer to her. Pretty soon, helping raise a newborn and working night shifts became too much, so he started taking business classes at a technical college instead—doing everything from delivering newspapers to buffing hospital floors to support his family.

And then he enrolled at Morehouse a second time. But even with a job, he couldn't keep up with the cost of tuition. So after getting his degree from that technical school, this father of three decided to come back to Morehouse for a third time. As Frederick says, "God has a plan or my life, and He's not done with me yet."

And today, Frederick is a family man, and a working man, and a Morehouse Man. And that's what I'm asking all of you to do: Keep settting an example for what it means to be a man. Be the best husband to your wife, or you're your boyfriend, or your partner. Be the best father you can be to your children. Because nothing is more important.

I was raised by a heroic single mom, wonderful grandparents—made incredible sacrifices for me. And I know there are moms and grandparents here today who did the same thing for all of you. And so my whole life, I've tried to be for Michelle and my girls what my father was not for my mother and me. I want to break that cycle where a father is not at home—where a father is not helping to raise that son or daughter. I want be a better father, a better husband, a better man.

It's hard work that demands your constant attention and frequent sacrifice. And I promise you, Michelle will tell you I'm not perfect. She's got a long list of my imperfections. Even now, I'm still practicing, I'm still learning, still getting corrected in terms of how to be a fine husband and a good father. But I will tell you this: Everything else is unfulfilled if we fail at family, if we fail at that responsibility.

I know that when I am on my deathbed someday, I will not be thinking about any particular legislation I passed; I will not be thinking about a policy I promoted; I will not be thinking about the speech I gave, I will not be thinking the Nobel Prize I received. I will be thinking about that walk I took with my daughters. I'll be thinking about a lazy afternoon with my wife. I'll be thinking about sitting around the dinner table and seeing them happy and healthy and knowing that they were loved. And I'll be thinking about whether I did right by all of them.

So be a good role model, set a good example for that young brother coming up. If you know somebody who's not on point, go back and bring that brother along—those who've been left behind, who haven't had the same opportunities we have—they need to hear from you. You've got to be engaged on the barbershops, on the basketball court, at church, spend time and energy and presence to give people opportunities and a chance. Pull them up, expose them, support their dreams. Don't put them down.

We've got to teach them just like what we have to learn, what it means to be a man—to serve your city like Maynard Jackson; to shape the culture like Spike Lee; to be like Chester Davenport, one of the first people to integrate the University of Georgia Law School. When he got there, nobody would sit next to him in class. But Chester didn't mind. Later on, he said, "It was the thing for me to do. Someone needed to be the first." And today, Chester is here celebrating his 50th reunion. Where is Chester Davenport? He's here.

So if you've had role models, father, brothers like that—thank them today. And if you haven't, commit yourself to being that man to somebody else.

And finally, as you do these things, do them not just for yourself, but don't even do them just for the African American community. I want to set your sights higher. At the turn of the last century, W.E.B. DuBois spoke about the "talented tenth"—a class of highly educated, socially conscious leaders in the black community. But it's not just the African American community that needs you. The country needs you. The world needs you.

As Morehouse Men, many of you know what it's like to be an outsider; know what it's like to be marginalized; know what it's like to feel the sting of discrimination. And that's an experience that a lot of Americans share. Hispanic Americans know that feeling when somebody asks them where they come from or tell them to go back. Gay and lesbian Americans feel it when a stranger passes judgment on their parenting skills or the love that they share. Muslim Americans feel it when they're stared at with suspicion because of their faith. Any woman who knows the injustice of earning less pay for doing the same work—she knows what it's like to be on the outside looking in.

So your experiences give you special insight that today's leaders need. If you tap into that experience, it should endow you with empathy—the understanding of what it's like to walk in somebody else's shoes, to see through their eyes, to know what it's like when you're not born on 3$^{rd}$ base, thinking you hit a triple. It should give you the ability to connect. It should give you a sense of compassion and what it means to overcome barriers.

And I will tell you, Class of 2013, whatever success I have achieved, whatever positions of leadership I have held depended less on Ivy League degrees or SAT scores or GPAs, and have instead been due to that sense of connection and empathy—the special obligation I felt, as a black man like you, to help those who need it most, people who didn't have the opportunities that I had—because there but for the grace of God, go I—I might have been in their shoes. I might have been in prison. I might have been unemployed. I might not have been able to support a family. And that motivates me.

So it's up to you to widen your circle of concern—to care about justice for everybody, white, black and brown. Everybody. Not just in your own community, but also across this country and around the world. To make sure everyone has a voice, and everybody gets a seat at the table; that everybody, no matter what you look like or where you come from, what your last name is—it doesn't matter, everybody gets a chance to walk through those doors of opportunity if they are willing to work hard enough.

When Leland Shelton was four years old—where's Leland? Stand up, Leland. When Leland Shelton was four years old, social services took him away from his mama, put him in care of his grandparents. By age 14, he was in the foster care system. Three years after that, Leland enrolled in Morehouse. And today he is graduating Phi Beta Kappa on his way to Harvard Law School. But he's not stopping there. As a member of the National Foster Care Youth and Alumni Policy Council, he plans to use his law degree to make sure kids like him don't fall through the cracks. And it won't matter whether they're black kids or brown kids or white kids or Native American kids, because he'll understand what they're going through. And he'll be fighting for them. He'll be in their corner. That's leadership. That's a Morehouse Man right there.

That's what we've come to expect from you, Morehouse—a legacy of leaders—not just in our black community, but for the entire American community. To recognize the burdens you carry with you, but to resist the temptation to use them as excuses. To transform the way we think about manhood, and set higher standards for ourselves and for others. To be successful, but also to understand that each of us has responsibilities not just to ourselves, but to one another and to future generations. Men who refuse to be afraid. Men who refuse to be afraid.

Members of the Class of 2013, you are heirs to a great legacy. You have within you that same courage and that same strength, the same resolve as the men who came before you. That's what being a Morehouse Man is all about. That's what being an American is all about.

Success may not come quickly or easily. But if you strive to do what's right, if you work harder and dream bigger, if you set an example in your own lives and do your part to help meet the challenges of our time, then I'm confident that, together, we will continue the never-ending task of perfecting our union.

Congratulations, Class of 2013. God bless you. God bless Morehouse. And God bless the United States of America.

# AND BARACK BECOMES A MOREHOUSE MAN!

U.S. President Barack Obama is presented with an honorary doctor of law degree by President of Morehouse College John Wilson after delivering the commencement address.

# EPILOGUE

Thank you, Barack Obama for 8 years of glorious service to America and to the world. If some decide to criticize and cast disrespect, I use the words of the Bible:

Ecclesiastes 9:7; "Go then, eat your bread in happiness and drink your wine with a cheerful heart, for God has already approved your works."

Respectfully yours,

Samuel Earl Wilson, III

# HALLELUJAH! GLORY!

*⌇*

"All is well that ends well," so the saying goes. The tenure in the White House often brings wealth afterwards, if not before. George Washington, our first president, (1789-1797) was worth $525 million; Thomas Jefferson, our third president (1801-1809), $212 million; Theodore Roosevelt, our 26th (1901-1909), $125 million; Andrew Jackson, our seventh (1829-1837), $119 million; and James Madison, our fourth (1809-1813), $101 million.

Those whose wealth were $1million or less: Harry Truman (1945-1953), William McKinley (1897-1901), Ulysses S. Grant (1869-1877), and Abraham Lincoln (1861-1865). Donald Trump will perhaps be the richest ever to serve.

The Obamas' net worth after leaving the oval office is perhaps $16.8 million. This figure includes $400,000 Wall Street speech, book signings, pension, royalties from books, etc.

In 2009, Obama said, "I did not run for office to be helping out a bunch of Fat Cat bankers on Wall Street." Never-the-less, as a black man, he is well blessed!

## ALL IS WELL WITH THE WORLD

Robert Browning in 1841 wrote in his poem, "Pippa Passes" these words:

The year's at the spring,
And day's at the morn;
Morning's at seven;
The hill-side's dew pearled;
The lark's on the wing
The snail's on the thorn
God's in his heaven -
All's right with the world!

I, Sam Wilson, wrote in my book <u>The Ghetto Poet</u>:

The frost is on the pumpkin.
The dew is on the ground.
The rainbow is in the sky
And the baby's sleeping sound.
The rent was paid yestidy,
And the groceries already made.
The calf's sucking its mother's titty,
And the dog's sleeping in the shade.
Our bellies are full with collard greens
And our thirsts are filled with brew.
Our pockets are filled with change,
What else is there to do?
I am satisfied!

Sam Wilson, III

# APPENDIX

On January 17, 1964, a star was born in the Black Ghetto of the city of Chicago, Illinois, a city founded by a Black man, a pioneer, Jean Baptiste point du Sable, in 1818. This is the city we Mississippians call "Mississippi, Illinois" because so many blacks from Mississippi have moved there. This beautiful Star's, the first Black First Lady of the United States of America, forefathers migrated not from Mississippi but from the Carolinas.

THE IMPECCABLE MICHELLE La VAUGHN OBAMA!!!

Yes, along came Michelle and with her came Class, Dignity, Beauty, Charm, and Intellect. Along came a woman of African heritage, more Sensuous than Cleopatra.

Ah, Shakespeare. If you were alive today, could you write the tale of Barack and Michelle as well as you did Anthony and Cleopatra?

And what about his wife, his spouse, his "old lady," the first Afro/American First Lady? Along came "Shell" or along came Michelle – Obama, that is.

I am a proponent of jazz music. What about you? I first became indoctrinated into the phenomena of jazz music at Morehouse College when Jose Ananias from New York City had probably the best collection of Jazz in the city of Atlanta, Georgia. Not that I was a stranger to black folks' music which I was accustomed to hearing like rhythm and blues, but jazz was something new and cool and "hep."

My New York buddies, Jose Ananias, Hank Butler and Clifton Hall discombobulated my musical mind by teaching me how to appreciate jazz. Jose had the best jazz collection in the whole city of Atlanta – in the whole wide world as far as I was concerned or knew. Instead of listening to Louis Jourdan, they introduced me to Charlie Parker – instead of Hawk Williams and Tennessee Ernie Ford, they substituted Ella Fitzgerald and Sarah Vaughn. B.B. King's and Buddy Guy's guitars were replaced by Charlie Christian's and Wes Montgomery's. Gradually I began to make my own choices. I substituted Thelonious Monk for Howling Wolf, Lester young instead of Fats Domino, Carmen McRae for Koko Taylor. Clifford Brown and Max Roach replaced Muddy Waters and Jimmy Reed. Coletrane for Buddy Johnson, and Dinah Washington for Ruth Brown.

I became cool not only in my walk but also in my talk - "Say, man, is this piano player we're going to see at the Walahaje Ofay?" The Walahaje was the source of our black pride. Not only was it a majestically beautiful building but it was built and owned by black entrepreneurs.

Years after my college days and teaching stints in Mississippi, I ventured to the state of New York's Rockland County to continue my occupation of teaching science and coaching. There in New York, along with my Jewish friend Jess Rosenstack, we enjoyed and were mesmerized by jazz to its utmost. We listened to and saw some of the greatest jazz men and women in existence. Jess was a jazz enthusiast and encyclopedian. With him, I saw Art Blakey and his Jazz Messengers perform Benny Golson's classic "Along Came Betty." I'm not a musician but it starts off like this: "da dum ker dum, repeat da dum ker dum." With Art Blakey setting the pace on drums, with Lee Morgan on trumpet transcending the scales with bliss, Benny Golson on tenor saxophone soothingly playing as if he had written it (he did), Bobby Timmons tickling the keys of the piano as though he had invented it, and Jimmie Merrit on bass timely accentuating the page genuinely, a star was born.

The song is smoother than Ben and Jerry's or Blue Bell or Borden's ice cream, as smooth as a sunset above the beach on a clear sky, and smoother than a single malt scotch itself. It makes one ask, "Who is this Betty?" I picture her as a beautiful, gracious, charming black female with a smile, dressed in expensive silk, walking as though she were floating on gorgeous, not skinny legs, on her way to lend her superior mind to solve problems too difficult for others to solve. She has been blessed by God with grace and dignity. The Jazz Messengers also played "Moaning." I believe she has the power to make you moan!

# THE CITY OF MICHELLE'S

I was perhaps 8 or 9 years of age when I first visited the city of Chicago, Illinois, the first real city of my life. New Orleans was only a hundred miles away, yet I'd never been there, nor had I been to Atlanta, the home of Morehouse College. These three cities I would visit over and over again as life dictated it to be.

Chicago fascinated me then and still fascinates me now. When we arrived by train, holding my mother's hand, I exclaimed out loud, "Mamma, these buildings are taller than the Forrest Hotel." For the fear of being embarrassed, she dragged me along and told me to shut up. The Forrest Hotel in Hattiesburg, Mississippi was the tallest building that I had ever seen. It stood five stories high.

Having read comic books and others, Chicago gave the thrills of fulfilling my dreams of drinking ice cream sodas like Archie, eating hamburgers like Wimpy of Popeye's, eating sundaes, hot dogs, milk shakes, and floats. Riding the "L's" trains, city buses, taxis, and Jitneys. The fairs and circus only came once a year down south but here in Chicago there was River View amusement park everyday if you could afford it. Even if you couldn't go everyday, there were always the green city parks that beckoned you to come with your baskets of food and drinks.

My Uncle Marvin's apartment was on the south side, the area of which produced Michelle LaVaughn Robinson, a place that if you were not black, you would be a minority. The only other ghettos I knew were called "Jew Town" and "Polish Town." Michelle's venture as a student at Princeton University was perhaps her first minority experience. Even then she graduated cum laude in her class of 1981, then on Harvard for her law degree. I'm not surprised because I had been taught long ago by my father that "You can find a black genius in the cotton fields of Mississippi."

Needless to say, we visited the Chicago Museum, Comiskey Park, Wrigley Field (where I saw Jackie Robinson play later when I was in high school).

My first city is and was a great city that produced America's first African/American First Lady!

*Her supreme Highness – You Go Girl – Foxy Mama!*

Duke Ellington must have had a clairvoyant premonition that Michelle Obama would be born 31 years later and in 2009 would become the first African-American First Lady when he coined the name of his classic hit *"SOPHISTICATED LADY"* in 1932-33. She is indeed the epitome of sophistication.

Although the lyrics, the words, DO NOT describe her, the music, the melody, do. "And when nobody is nigh, SHE DOES NOT CRY, she has Barack Obama as her Knight in shining armor."

### THE BEAUTIFUL SOPHISTICATED LADY!

This is how I picture the first black, colored, First Lady – Michelle LaVaughn Robinson Obama. What a beautiful creature she is. Barack is blessed to have her. The 44th First Lady.

Please notice the not so skinny legs.

# TODAY, TOMORROW, FOREVER?

There is a book titled *Year Million*. It makes you think and wonder if you could trade your present life for a life one million years from now, with the rapid progress of science and technology of today, how precious life would be in a million years?

1. Would cancer be a thing of the past, something that once was or used to be?
2. Would hate have been replaced by love?
3. Would all hospitals become rest resorts?
4. With the advancement of medicines, how long would your life span be?
5. Would science labs become churches and places of worship or would places of worship be transformed to science labs?
6. Would love and marriage still exist or would the uniting of people be a computerized selection of couples?
7. How long would a journey be across the world and how long would it take for a trip from Mississippi to New York or California?
8. Would there still be hurricanes, tornadoes, cyclones, destructive storms, forest fires, droughts and famines, or will man have mastered all of these?
9. Will mankind love his neighbor as himself and war be only a word in the history books?
10. And then, YOU, a million years from now, wonder what life would be a million years from then????

Samuel Earl Wilson, III

And will the legacy of the first black president of the United States of America, Barack Obama, still be remembered? Will you be remembered? Will I?

# ADDENDUMS-ACCOMPLISHMENTS-ACHIEVEMENTS (11)

Some folks will agree with me and some will disagree, yet I have chosen eleven accolades as Barack Obama's greatest:

1. He got the attention of Morehouse College, delivered the commencement address in 2013 and was bestowed the honor of becoming a Morehouse Man. One star below Dr. Martin Luther King, Jr.

2. He passed the Health Care Reform. These presidents – Franklin Roosevelt, Dwight Eisenhower, John Kennedy, Lyndon Johnson, Richard Nixon, and Jimmy Carter – did not succeed in their missions to do so. 13 million uninsured Americans can now sigh in relief and not agony.

3. He ended the war in Iraq. He pulled all our military forces out by December 18, 2011, giving some troops a happy Hanukkah and a Merry Christmas.

4. He kicked some asses, by restoring integrity to America. Toppled Muammar Gaddafi in 2011, rescued Captain Phillips from Somali's pirates, and did not cry "Vengeance is mine, said the Lord." To Osama Bin Laden, but "NI" (in the words of the ghetto) -Now, I got you back, Mother F.

5. He saved the U.S. Auto Industry by using 60 billion in federal money plus $13.4 billion in loans left over from the Bush administration to General Motors and Chrysler.

6. He was pro-scientific. Expanded stem cell research, favoring treatments for spinal injuries. Perhaps the victims can overcome their handicaps and become normal again.

7. He reestablished U.S.-Cuba relationships. For the first time in 54 years, the American flag is flown in Cuba.

8. He was a prodigy of renewable technology. Investing $90 billion – electric cars, renewable electricity generators, clean coal, etc.

9. He was a proponent of quality education in America. Not only did he challenge the students to find themselves and their aspirations in their lives but to endure and strive for excellency in classes of no interest to them now (perhaps in the future?), but also to their teachers to qualify themselves to impart knowledge.

10. He was Salubrious. Favorable to or promoting health or well being. Not only himself but his spouse has the same concerns.

11. **HE MADE US PROUD, NO MATTER THE COLOR OF OUR SKIN – THE OTHER LANGUAGE WE SPEAK, THE RELIGION WE PRACTICE. <u>ASANTE - MERCI beaucoup – DANKE - GRACIAS!</u>**

Printed in the United States
By Bookmasters